Home Is Where Your Horse Is

Dandi Daley Mackall

CPH.
SAINT LOUIS

Horsefeathers

Horsefeathers!
Horse Cents
Horse Whispers in the Air
A Horse of a Different Color
Horse Angels
Home Is Where Your Horse Is

Interest level: ages 12–16

Scripture quotations are taken from the HOLY BIBLE, NEW INTER-
NATIONAL VERSION®. NIV®. Copyright © 1973, 1978, 1984 by
International Bible Society. Used by permission of Zondervan
Publishing House. All rights reserved.

Text Copyright © 2000 Dandi Daley Mackall
Published by Concordia Publishing House
3558 S. Jefferson Avenue, St. Louis, MO 63118-3968
Manufactured in the United States of America

1 2 3 4 5 6 7 8 9 10   09 08 07 06 05 04 03 02 01 00

This one is for my agent and friend,

Elizabeth Frost Knappman of New

England Publishing Associates. You

are absolutely the best!

1

Spring hit hard at Horsefeathers. Although we had two full months left of our freshman year, I couldn't remember ever feeling so restless. Maybe all I had was a bad case of spring fever, but it sure felt like more.

"Scoop?" Maggie 37 Brown raised the volume on her fake Southern accent, the one she was perfecting for her theater career. "Are you even listening to me?" She hoisted her saddle on the back of Moby, her old white mare. "I said, we should have a Mother's Day parade. It wouldn't raise money, but Horsefeathers Stable would get a lot of free publicity."

I brushed Orphan's sleek, black coat. She'd already shed her winter shag. Orphan's warm, earthy smell was the one thing in my life that never changed.

"I hate Mother's Day, Maggie," I said, not risking a glance at my best friend.

"Why, Sarah Coop!" she scolded. "Nobody hates Mother's Day! Isn't that unAmerican or something? *My* mother gave me the middle name *37*, plus she acts like she loves my little stepbrothers better than me, and *I* don't hate Mother's Day."

I grinned at Maggie. She had no idea what it felt like to be motherless. My parents adopted me when I was 3, then died when I was 7. It had been eight years since then, eight Mother's Days. And I'd hated every one of them. "Let's talk about it later, Maggie," I said. "At the next Horsefeathers meeting?"

Orphan nudged me with her soft, velvet muzzle. *She* understood. Her mom had died when she was foaled.

Moby didn't want the bit in her mouth. Maggie reached up and down as her clever mare dodged the bridle. "Well," Maggie said, making a quick move that landed the bit in Moby's mouth, "Mother's Day is in two weeks. We can't wait too long to start planning for the parade. I want the whole town to get involved, and that takes—"

Maggie was interrupted by the thunder of galloping hooves and a cry from outside the barn. "Whoa! Hey! Scoop! Where are you?"

"That sounds like Stephen Dalton," Maggie said, tightening the saddle strap.

"If you're in there, come outside!"

No denying it. It was definitely Stephen Dalton, the person I'd least like to see, even when I'm not in a rotten mood. His dad owns Dalton

Stables and half our county.

"We could hide?" Maggie suggested.

I sighed. "I'm here, Stephen!" I shouted. "If you want me, you can come in here."

Stephen Dalton would never drop by Horsefeathers unless he wanted something. According to him, Dalton Stables is the only *real* stables in the county, and my stable, Horsefeathers, isn't much more than a barn.

Curiosity finally getting to me, I walked Orphan around to the front of the barn, where Stephen was trying to dismount his prizewinning sorrel gelding.

"Whoa, Champion!" he yelled, jerking back the reins on his English bridle. "Hold still!"

"Is this some kind of show horse routine?" I asked, leaning against my own horse, who may not be a registered, purebred show horse, but is more of a friend than Stephen's horse would ever be.

"You have to come with me to the stables," Stephen said.

Like "the stables" had to mean *his* stables.

"Excuse me?" I gave him my baffled look. "I *am* at the stables." I turned to Maggie, and she was holding in a laugh. Her dark brown skin looked nearly black next to Moby's bright white coat.

"Scoop!" Stephen whined. "To Dalton Stables."

I faced him. "Why would I want to go

there?" Annoying Stephen was turning out to be the highlight of my day.

"Will you quit being dense?" Stephen said. "Or don't you care what happens to that *miracle* filly?" He said it like miracles were childish.

I knew Stephen was talking about the foal Jen and I had helped deliver when we were snowbound at Dalton's over Thanksgiving. The filly had been as unexpected as the snow, and we'd almost lost her. That had been almost five months ago. Since then, I'd kept so busy at Horsefeathers I hadn't gotten back to see the foal as often as I'd wanted. But I did visit a few times a week because I knew nobody else at Dalton's would think it was important enough just to hang out with her.

"I don't believe for one minute that you care enough about that filly to ride over here, Stephen." But even as I said it, I knew *I* cared. I cared enough to feel that queasy feeling in my stomach that something could be wrong with her.

"Okay then," he said, pretending to turn his horse toward Dalton's. "I'll tell the new owner I was wrong, and you really don't care."

"You sold them?" I asked. I knew they'd sell the mare and filly eventually. I'd been praying they'd go to a good home. "Out with it, Stephen! Is something wrong with Lefty?"

"Lefty?" Stephen looked like he'd just swallowed dirt.

In my head I'd called the filly Lefty because she'd tried to be born left foreleg first. That's what had caused all her trouble being born. "The filly?" I pressed.

Stephen got his serious look back. "They're trying to load her with the mare, but she won't load. The owner's afraid she'll—"

I didn't hear anything else. "Maggie!" I called, as I swung up on Orphan bareback. "Lefty's in trouble."

2

Orphan and I almost ran over Stephen and Champion as we galloped away from Horsefeathers. Behind me, I heard Moby's thundering hooves and Stephen whining about something. But I couldn't see anything except Orphan's swirling black mane in my face as I leaned forward. And after a few minutes, I couldn't hear anything but the spring wind rushing past us as Orphan jumped the fence and raced across Dalton land.

Just over the hill Dalton Stables came into view, hogging a whole field and taking up more room than the Kentucky Derby. In the side paddock, several people were huddled in a tight circle. Beside them I recognized Lefty's mother, the chestnut thoroughbred, Dream. But something was wrong. She squealed, a plugged-up whinny full of terror.

"They've twitched her, Orphan!" I muttered. One of the Dalton grooms held the bat-shaped twitch with a loop of rope sticking out of it. The loop was twisted around the mare's muzzle to make her do what they wanted.

I didn't need to urge Orphan on. She raced faster and faster toward the paddock fence. Several feet from the mare, Ralph Dalton and the others seemed to be staring down at something in the middle of them. A high squeal shot from the center of their circle. It was Lefty! They had her pinned to the ground.

My stomach knotted. Now I could see Lefty lying on her side, squirming as they tried to hog-tie her legs.

"Go, Orphan!" I whispered. I leaned forward and knew she read my heart. I gripped with my knees and thighs as we rose in the air, jumping the white board fence, clearing it by a foot.

We thudded inside Dalton paddock and kept going—straight for Lefty. Startled faces turned toward us. Somebody yelled, "Stop her!"

A horse's length away from them, I whispered, "Whoa." Orphan stiffened her legs and slid to a stop inches from Ralph Dalton. I swung my leg over and jumped from my horse. In one step I was at Lefty's side.

"Get away from her!" I shouted, shoving arms and legs out of my way.

Somebody fell back in the dirt.

A few feet away, Lefty's mom squealed and jerked against the twitch. I stormed over to her, grabbed the hateful twitch out the groom's hands, untwisted the rope loop from the mare's muzzle, and let her breathe. She nickered her thanks, then pawed nervously. I knew how much she loved her baby.

"Sarah!" shouted Ralph Dalton. "I don't know what you think you're—"

"Everybody just stand back!" I commanded, dropping the twitch and rushing back to Lefty's side.

"Who is she?" asked a woman, getting to her feet and slapping dust off her blue jeans. She must have been the one I'd knocked over getting to Lefty. I didn't care.

"Now listen to me, Sarah," Stephen's dad said, not coming any closer as I untied the rough rope from Lefty's forelegs. "We're not hurting the foal. Ms. Twopennies needs to get both horses into her trailer. She's come to take them home. We were just—"

"It's okay, Lefty," I murmured, wishing everybody in the world would just go away. "I won't let them hurt you. That's a good girl."

The rope had already left hairless marks on her narrow pasterns, just above the hoof. They had probably left emotional marks too. She might never trust these people again, which was fine with me.

I threw the rope as far away as I could. Whispering to Lefty, I scratched her ears where I knew she liked it. Her little chest heaved in and out in quick, sharp breaths.

I scratched her back until she stopped trembling. Out of the corner of my eye, I saw watchful Orphan guarding both of us, and Maggie 37 keeping Moby at a distance so she wouldn't interfere. At least one human had good horse sense.

With my arm around her neck, Lefty followed my lead and got to her feet.

I turned to the mare and whistled. She came trotting over to me. I let the mare check out her foal, nuzzling her and nipping her gently. Lefty was lucky to have such a good mom, and Dream was lucky to have Lefty.

Ralph Dalton was making some kind of apology to the woman, who must have been the new owner. I felt her gaze stick on me like botflies to horse hair, even when Stephen—on foot—joined his dad.

I didn't know where the owner would be taking her horses, but it was bound to be more horse-friendly than Dalton Stables. I wondered if I would ever see Lefty again. Since I'd just knocked her owner into the dirt, probably not. My throat burned with tears I wouldn't give any of the humans the satisfaction of seeing.

A black, four-horse trailer sat, tail ramp down, ready for its cargo. I liked the trailer. Someone had sprinkled straw on the floor and left plenty of room for the horses by taking out the middle divider. At least I could help Lefty and her mother get used to the trailer.

"Okay, Girls," I said. "Shall we?"

Ralph Dalton protested. "Wait just a minute—"

"No, let her alone." I didn't look back, but it was a woman's voice, probably the owner's.

I walked to the trailer, and both horses followed me closely. When I stepped up the ramp, they did too. Calmly, I snapped a lead rope on the mare so she wouldn't shift her weight too much on the road.

That was the easy part. Now I had to face *people*. I said a quick prayer, a general call for help, and walked out of the trailer.

When I came out, they were all staring at me. "Horsefeathers," I said. "Did I hurt anybody?"

Stephen stood next to his dad. Twin Dalton glares aimed double-barreled disapproval at me. Too bad.

The woman stepped toward me. She was slim, taller than I am, maybe 5'6", and about twice as pretty as anybody I'd ever seen. Her black hair was pulled back in a long braid. That and her dark skin, deep brown eyes, and high cheek bones, made me think she might be part American Indian. If she'd been a horse, she might have been a Paint or an Appaloosa, steady and quietly capable.

"Yeah, I'm hurt," she said. But her eyes seemed to be closer to a smile than to anything else as they narrowed in on me. "How did you do that?"

I opened my mouth, but nothing came out.

Maggie and Moby trotted up to my rescue. Moby reared, and Maggie bowed. "How do y'all do?" she said. "I'm Maggie 37 Blue. Born on March 7—third month, seventh day—get it? My middle name was given to me by my mother, who holds that 37 is her lucky number."

She didn't bother explaining that although her last name is really Brown, she picks stage names to go along with whatever color she's wearing. Today, Maggie 37 *Blue*. Yesterday, Maggie 37 *Green*.

Maggie waved her arm in my direction. "And this is Sarah Coop, better known as Scoop. In case you haven't heard, she's the best horse gentler in the entire world, owner of the world-famous Horsefeathers Stable."

Leave it to Maggie.

"World famous?" Stephen gave a fake laugh that sounded like a horse coughing. "Horsefeathers is more like a barn than a stable."

I swallowed and tried to speak for myself. "I'm sorry ... about pushing you. I just couldn't stand to see the mare twitched—"

"I told you not to do that, Ralph." The woman spoke in a normal tone, but her voice meant business, and Ralph Dalton's face flushed. "You should have listened to me."

She walked up and shook my hand. "Twila Twopennies," she said. She smelled like violets. "Now would you like to tell me how you managed to load those horses, when the lot of us couldn't get them near the trailer?"

I shrugged. "I guess I get along a whole lot better with horses than with people." I smiled weakly over at Stephen's dad, but he didn't even pretend to smile back. "I've been hanging out with Lefty from Day One. She's just used to me."

Twila Twopennies laughed. It made her look like a good-natured quarter horse. "Why do you call her Lefty?"

"Didn't they tell you?" I asked. "When she was foaled, my friend Jen and my brother B.C. and I were snowbound here. The foal tried to come out with her left foot first. I had to reach in and pull the other hoof out."

She turned to Stephen Dalton. "Stephen, you said *you* were the one who delivered that filly."

He kicked up a cloud of dirt and didn't look at her. "Whatever."

Twila Twopennies walked to her trailer and checked her horses.

Stephen came up behind me and whispered, "I don't know what you're trying to do, but it won't do you any good." I shivered as his spit sprayed my neck. "Don't you have work to do at your own little barn? Quit trying to show off here. Just go back to your backyard horses where you belong."

I moved away from Stephen. Maggie smiled sadly at me. She knew what saying good-bye to Lefty was doing to me. I watched as the woman closed the tail gate, sealing in the horses. The thought of never seeing Lefty again made me bite my lip until I tasted blood.

3

I swung myself up on Orphan's bare back, anxious to get out of there before my tears broke loose. I'd always known Lefty wouldn't be around forever, but it still felt like they were squeezing her out of my heart.

"Wait a minute!" Twila Twopennies shouted from the trailer. "Scoop?"

I pivoted Orphan to face her.

"Could you ... would you mind riding with me and helping me unload these two? They seem pretty fond of you."

"*I'll* go," Stephen said, stepping in front of Orphan and me.

"That's okay, Stephen," she said. "I'm sure your dad can use you here."

Ralph Dalton shrugged. I could tell he didn't like the way this was shaping up any more than his son did.

"Answer her, Scoop," Maggie whispered, riding up next to me. "I can take Orphan back. Go! Do it."

"I could drive you back once the horses are

settled," Twila Twopennies said. "I'll pay you for your time, of course."

"You don't need to do that," I said, once I was finally able to get the words in my head to exit my mouth, a distance that felt as long as a racetrack. "Thanks for asking. I'd like to help get Lefty settled." I slid off Orphan and handed Maggie the reins.

"Good," Ms. Twopennies said, getting back into the cab of her truck.

Maggie leaned down and whispered to me. "Isn't it just too weird!"

"I think it's a good idea," I said, patting Orphan good-bye.

"No, I mean *her!*" Maggie's whisper made me uncomfortable. I wondered if Twila T. would think we were talking about her—which, I guess, we were.

"She's not so bad," I said. "She didn't—"

"Scoop!" Maggie cut me off. "I *mean* the way she looks! It's totally eerie how she looks exactly like you, only older. Don't you think it's weird? I got goosebumps."

The horn honked, and I jogged to the trailer. Maggie was the one who was weird. True, I'd wondered if this woman might be part American Indian. And I'd always imagined that I had real American Indian blood in me. Since I never knew anything about my biological parents, I used to pretend I was an Indian princess. My skin and hair are dark enough. Hers were too. But Twila Twopennies was beautiful. And I'm not.

"Maggie!" I called over my shoulder before I jumped in the passenger seat. "Call Dotty and tell her I'll be home late." Then I remembered. It was Saturday. Dotty would be working late at the Hy-Klas Grocery Store. "Scratch that!" I shouted. "Dotty's working. Bye, Maggie!"

The engine started, and I hopped in, all of a sudden realizing I had no idea where I was going.

"Don't you want to know where you're going?" Twila Twopennies asked as if I'd just said out loud what I was thinking. She backed the trailer, keeping the axle straight. "We're going to Cherokee Bend."

"Cherokee Bend?" I'd heard of the place, a riding camp for rich kids. "But Lefty's mother, Dream, she's not a riding horse. She's got to be a racehorse." I was sure that mare wouldn't have made a good trail horse or a lesson horse for greenhorn kids. Was that the kind of life I was taking Lefty and her mother to?

"Relax, Scoop," Twila said. She wheeled the trailer onto the highway. "Cherokee Bend is a lot more than the riding camps. We've put out quite a few racing thoroughbreds, including a couple of champions. Dream should make a good broodmare, if Lefty is an example of what she's capable of producing."

"Do you board your horses there all year round?" I asked, feeling a little better.

She grinned. "I own Cherokee Bend. And in case you're wondering, I'm half Cherokee and half Irish."

I stared out the rolled-down window and felt the cool breeze. It smelled like spring and dandelions. Some of the yellow dandelions were already sprouting in ditches. Everybody else calls them weeds, but I've always loved the way they can be pretty anyway, blooming where they land, as if they don't care what people think about them.

"Look at those dandelions!" Twila Twopennies exclaimed as we passed a huge patch of yellow. She said it like she thought they were pretty.

Weird. Now I knew someone else who liked dandelions.

We drove a while without talking. I knew Maggie would have kept up a lively conversation if she'd been there. Maggie is like a Lipizzaner performing horse. I'm more like your Standard Bred.

"How far is your ranch from here, Mrs. Twopennies?" It was the best attempt at conversation I could muster.

"*Ms.* Twopennies," she corrected. She turned down a bumpy side road. "You can call me Twila," she said. "Actually, this is already my land. We turned onto Twopennies Lane about a half-mile back."

"Horsefeathers!" I said, staring out at the winter oats and the fields that would soon be mowed for hay. There was nothing but fields and pastures as far as I could see on either side.

Twila laughed, but not a mocking Stephen Dalton laugh. "Where did such a young girl pick up such an old expression? I haven't heard anybody say 'horsefeathers' in longer than I care to remember."

"I guess I got it from my grandfather," I said, a twinge of sadness still springing up from somewhere deep inside me when I thought about Grandad. It hadn't even been a year since he died.

"At least now I know where you got the name for Horsefeathers Stable." She glanced at me, then into the rearview mirror. "I have a feeling you're a great help to your parents with the horses. Does your father own the stable or manage it? Or your grandfather?"

I stared out the window as fence posts swept by. The road had turned to dirt and gravel, jogging us to slow down. "No, I run the stable. It's mine."

I felt her stare, but I kept looking out at the fields.

"I don't understand," she said. "Did your parents give you—"

"I don't have parents," I said, not quite sure if I'd said it out loud or just in my head.

"Scoop, I'm sorry," Twila said, sounding sorry, but not pitying. "I didn't know. Do you live with your grandparents then?"

I shook my head. "They're dead too," I said. "Me and B.C., my brother—he's in fourth grade—we live with Dotty, our aunt."

She didn't ask me a million questions, which may have been why I kept talking.

"My parents died when I was 7." I thought about saying *My adoptive parents died when I was seven,* but that seemed too confusing. Besides, Emma and Ben Coop had been the only parents I'd ever known.

"B.C. was just two," I continued. "That's B.C., for *Bottle Cap,* 'cause he's loved bottle caps forever, which is where my folks worked—the bottle cap plant. Anyway, Dad worked the day shift, and Mom took nights. But sometimes she'd go in a little early so she could see my dad before she started her shift. And she was in early the day the plant had an explosion. A lot of people got hurt, but they were the only two people killed."

"And you moved in with your aunt?" she asked, her voice soft as feathers. "Does she help you with the stables?"

I laughed. "Not Dotty. She likes horses to look at, but I don't think she's ever been on one. Maggie—you met her—and Jen Zucker and Carla Buckingham help out at Horsefeathers. Besides, Dotty's got her hands full with B.C."

I stopped. Why was I rattling on like this? I hadn't known Twila very long, and already I'd told her more than I'd told anybody except my best friends. She didn't need to hear all about my brother's manic depression though. I shut up.

"Here we are," she said. We pulled up a lane horses would enjoy walking over—soft, firm dust and sawdust mix. The stable was big, but not showy, with a long horse barn and pastures on all sides.

"That's where we give our beginner lessons," Twila said, pointing to a good-sized arena on one side of the long barn. The ring was big enough that horses wouldn't get bored too fast walking in circles.

The paddock looked perfectly groomed, as if somebody had mowed it, but the pastures out back were wild and dotted with horses grazing to their hearts' content. It wasn't a place Orphan would have been happy, but as far as commercial stables go, this one looked like one of the best and most horse-friendly I'd ever run across.

Twila pulled the trailer up next to the barn. "Scoop, will you get the lead rope for me. I think it's in the backseat." She got out, and I popped my seatbelt and leaned over to look for the rope in the backseat. It was on the floor. I stretched to reach it.

Outside, I heard the latch open and the back tailgate ramp drop to the ground. Then I heard a man's voice: "I'll scare them out, Twila."

No way was anybody going to scare Lefty out! I grabbed the rope and struggled out of the truck and back to the trailer. Somebody was starting up the ramp. All I could see were his blue jeans, but he was heading for Lefty.

"Wait!" I cried. "Don't scare them! I'll lead them out."

He stopped at the head of the ramp, pivoted like a cutting horse, and frowned down at me from the shadow of the trailer. "Twila, who is this?"

"This is Scoop," Twila said matter-of-factly.

"Tell her to get out the way before she gets hurt. I'm fixing to run these two down the ramp."

I stepped up on the ramp, taking it in two strides until I was nose to nose with him, or rather my nose to his chest. "If *you'll* just get out of the way, I can lead both of them down."

"I suppose you plan to lead the filly too?"

"Yes." My eyes were adjusting to the dark of the trailer. I could see that this guy was only a couple of years older than me.

"Yeah, well, sorry. I need to trap the filly, or we'll never catch her. I'm not going to hurt them." He turned away, as if he were going through with his plan.

"Wait—" I reached for him and caught hold of his shirt. My foot slipped on the ramp and I lost my balance.

"Hey!" he yelled.

Before I knew what was happening, I was tumbling backwards, down the trailer ramp. But my fingers wouldn't let go of the shirt. The cowboy came tumbling down with me.

My seat bounced on the dirt. I fell backwards, rolled over, kicking and spitting out the dirt that filled my mouth. When I stopped rolling, I opened my eyes.

I was lying on top of the best-looking cowboy I'd ever seen.

4

I stared into his huge, brown eyes. I'd always believed Jen's brother Travis to be the most handsome guy in the world. Maggie said he was. But this leathery, tan-skinned cowboy with his thick, curly black hair would give even Travis a run for his money.

"Do you mind?" His voice was deep as a well, as hypnotic as his eyes. When I didn't move, he cleared his throat. His eyebrows arched, and a dimple poked his left cheek.

"Horsefeathers!" I muttered, suddenly fully aware where I was, that I had him pinned in the dirt. I stumbled to my feet and brushed the dust from my jeans.

He got up and dusted himself off. His brown-and-black checked shirt had the sleeves ripped off, probably by the enormous shoulders that poked out. If he'd been a horse, he might have been a Lusitano, the muscle-bound horses ridden by Portuguese bullfighters.

"What was that all about?" he asked, taking a step toward me.

I stepped back. "I—I'm—" Nothing else came out.

Twila appeared beside me. I'd almost forgotten about her. "Are you two all right?" she asked. "Colt," she said, looking to him as she put a hand on my shoulder. "I was trying to introduce you to Scoop, Sarah Coop. She helped our new mare, Dream, deliver her foal at Dalton Stables. Remember, I told you it was a tough delivery?"

He nodded.

"Scoop," Twila said, "this cantankerous cowboy is my right-hand man, Colt Cleveland. He gives lessons, watches the broodmares, and does a little bit of everything else around here. And with that introduction, I think I'll leave you to it. Put Dream and her foal—Lefty—in the south pasture by themselves for the night. I'm going to fix us something to drink. Think you can manage without me?"

"No problem, Ma'am," Colt said.

Twila walked off across the lawn. I watched her go and for the first time noticed her house. I don't know how I could have missed it. It was huge, built like a log cabin, with big cathedral windows in front and glass all around.

When I looked back at Colt, he was staring at me. I felt my face heat up. "Sorry," I muttered.

He didn't say anything, but cocked his head and bowed, sweeping his arm toward the trailer—a *go ahead, after you* gesture.

I took him up on the offer, glad to get back to four-legged creatures where I felt more at ease. I stepped up into the trailer, untied Dream and scratched Lefty's ears. Whispering, so we wouldn't be overheard, I said, "Come on, mother and daughter. Let's show this cowboy a thing or two."

The mare backed down the ramp with no problem, reaching the yard in four quick steps. Lefty pranced head-first after her.

As soon as they hit earth, Lefty tore off to explore. The Daltons had already weaned her from her mother, and she was independent enough to set out on her own. She kicked up her heels and trotted to the water trough. With her muzzle, she splashed, then darted away as if some mysterious sea creature had sprayed her with water.

Colt took the mare's lead rope out of my hands. "That filly is going to be impossible to catch now. I'll take Dream. How you plan to capture *Lefty*, that's up to you."

I watched him lead Dream through a gate into a small paddock, where two bays grazed peacefully. They jerked up their heads and nickered a greeting. Dream answered them.

Colt opened another gate to a lush pasture that looked empty. It was a good sign that Twila intended to give the horses the run of the pasture all night. Not many stables would have had the sense to let the horses stay outside all night, much less allow them time to get used to the stable grounds without interference from other horses.

Colt turned and gave me a *so-why-haven't-you-caught-that-filly-yet* shrug.

"Lefty?" I called.

The filly twisted her little body that still had a gray fluffy carpet look. She hadn't finished her romp yet.

I walked up to her. "Don't make me look bad now," I said. "Don't you want to play in a bigger, greener pasture with your mom."

When I said *mom*, something pinged inside of me, like when you flick a speck of eraser dust off a piece of paper. Maybe it was because I didn't have to say the word, the name, the job—*mom*—very often. Maybe it was because *Mom*'s Day was so close. I shook it off.

Kneeling in the dirt about three feet away from Lefty, I watched as she sniffed a dandelion next to the fence. She lipped it, without pulling it out of the ground and seemed surprised when it moved.

"Lefty," I called.

As if she'd just that second noticed me, she trotted to me and lipped my hair that hung just about to my waist.

Slowly, I put my arms around her neck in a firm hug. Then I stood up and walked toward the south pasture. I'd practiced leading Lefty at Dalton Stables. When I kept one arm over her neck, she followed as closely as if I'd held her by a halter and lead rope.

Colt stood at the gate to the south pasture, holding it open far enough for Lefty and me to squeeze in. I stopped in front of him, and Lefty stopped too, waiting until I told her it was all right.

Colt grinned down with white teeth that would have made Maggie 37 swoon. "How did you do that?" he asked, each word released separately from his lips, without breaking his smile.

Shrugging, I glanced down at my feet. I'd worn my worst, my oldest living boots. I hadn't planned on seeing anybody but Maggie and the horses. His boots were well worn like real boots should be. But even dusty and scuffed, it was easy to tell they were top-level, fine leather boots.

"So, you work some kind of magic up there at Dalton Stables?" he asked.

"I don't have anything to do with Dalton Stables," I said, too quickly and too loud. "I keep horses at Horsefeathers—" For some reason it didn't seem right to say *Horsefeathers Stables*. Not compared to Cherokee Bend. "I was just at the Daltons when Dream dropped her foal. So I got an early start with her, I guess."

I led Lefty around him and through the

gate. She trotted in, playfully bucking, then making a bee-line to her mother.

"What do you mean 'an early start with her'?" Colt closed the gate after me.

"Like geese," I said.

"Geese?" He sounded skeptical.

"Or ducks?" I said, trying to remember how Jen had explained it to me. "My friend Jen Zucker read about how sometimes geese bond with dogs or cats or people. Whatever is in front of them when the babies hatch out of their eggs, that's what they bond with. This one goose thought a collie was its mother and followed that dog everywhere, even chasing cars."

He laughed and waited for more.

I wished Jen could have been there to explain.

"Anyway, I was there for Lefty, when she came into the world."

"So Lefty thinks you're her mother?" he asked. I couldn't tell for sure, but I think he was teasing.

"No," I said, not looking directly at him because I knew I wouldn't be able to talk at all if I did. "Lefty knows Dream is her mother. She's just close to me because I was there too. And because I messed with her for her first few hours of life."

The breeze picked up and blew my hair across my face so I had to shove it back. I glimpsed his big, brown eyes, intent on me, as if he were really listening.

"How? How did you mess with her?" he asked.

I laughed. If I told him, he'd probably really think I was nuts. "Okay, but don't laugh."

He grinned as he held up two fingers in a mock salute.

"I picked the foal up and carried her around. It's something I learned from my grandad, who learned it from his dad. To tell you the truth, Grandad didn't always raise his horses the way I would. He didn't gentle them like we do at Horsefeathers. But he'd always pick up new foals and carry them around."

"Did he tell you why?" He reached over and pulled something out of my hair, a long piece of hay.

I swallowed hard and nodded. "My grandad's dad used to farm with Percherons. You know Percherons?"

"Good plow horses," he said. "Huge. Horses don't come any bigger."

"Right. But my great-grandad claimed that after he picked up a foal, no matter how old it got or how big, that horse would always do whatever he said because it believed that my skinny great-grandad could pick it up and carry it around whenever he felt like it."

He burst into a hearty laugh that reminded

me of fireworks.

A bell clanged back up by the house.

"That's for us," Colt said, checking the gate latch. He took off running out of the paddock toward the house.

There didn't seem to be much else I could do but run after him, although I had no idea where I was going or what I was getting myself into.

5

The big bell clanged again as I ran across the paddock to catch up with Colt. I couldn't help thinking of the old "Bonanza" reruns B.C. and Dotty watched sometimes. The cook on "Bonanza" rang a dinner bell to call in the ranch hands.

Colt slowed to a fast walk, and I fell in beside him. I wished I didn't look so ragged, that I'd at least taken time to put on a clean shirt or brush my hair more.

I tried to remember when I'd first heard of Cherokee Bend. "Has Twila lived here long?" I asked.

"Yes and no," Colt said. "My dad knew her in high school. They both went to Claremont. On their graduation night, Twila ran off with some kid from Kennsington. She was gone for a long time, years. I think she got married. Dad said there were rumors that she had a baby. But when she moved back here about five years ago, she was by herself. And she started the ranch all by herself too."

I didn't like gossip, but I had a million questions I'd have liked to ask. How could she have started the ranch alone? What happened to her husband? What happened to her baby?

One side of Twila's lawn was lined with bright yellow bushes, snuggled next to each other and smelling like clover. I followed Colt up a little stone path to the side of the house, past huge beds of tulips spread out like a red carpet.

I'd always thought that if I ever took time to plant flowers, I'd plant tulips and they'd all be red, just like these.

A glass door slid back, and Twila nodded us in with a tilt of her head. She'd changed into a long, straight, silky dress with tiny straps that showed how tan she was, or how dark-skinned. I'd never seen anybody walk like she did, without moving anything, it seemed, except her feet.

"Come into the kitchen," she said, gliding across the floor that was real wood. The house smelled like pine—not a fake pine cleaner, but real forest pine. I don't know much about houses, but this one looked like a cross between a ranch house or log house and some kind of fancy ski lodge. Windows looked out on pastures and trees and horses as far as I could see in every direction.

We walked through a giant room with an entire wall made of stone and a stone fireplace that looked big enough to burn whole trees.

"Thirsty?" Twila asked, not waiting for an answer.

Colt slid into what looked like a restaurant booth, except the backs were wagon wheels and the seats real leather that whooshed when I slid in across from him.

Twila put tall, clear glasses in front of us. They were so cold, frost had formed on the outside of the glass. Each one had a green-and-white striped straw and a slice of lime floating on the top. Instead of setting the glasses right on the table, she set out small, green napkins first. "Hope you like limeade," she said.

"I do!" I said, surprised. I wasn't kidding. I *love* limeade. It's just that I didn't know anybody else liked it. Dotty never made limeade. B.C. said it tasted like horse sweat. But whenever we ate out, which was only a couple of times a year at best, I'd order limeade.

Colt took a big gulp from his glass, ignoring the straw. "If you don't like limeade, you better learn to like it—if you plan on coming around here much." He grinned easily at Twila, who returned the grin.

Maggie already would have found out how old Colt was, how old Twila was, their pasts, presents, and futures. I couldn't guess their ages. I thought Colt was probably Travis' age, 16 pushing 17. But I'm rotten at guessing people's ages. I could have nailed the age of every horse on the property, give or take a year, with one good look in the horse's mouth. But people are a different matter. And you can't exactly go around inspecting the shape and number of their teeth.

"So, Scoop," Twila said, sliding in next to Travis. "What do you think?"

"It's great," I said, downing half of my limeade with two long draws on the striped straw. It was so cold, my head ached.

Twila laughed gently. "Not the limeade. Cherokee Bend? My ranch?"

I set my glass down on the thick, green napkin. "It's great. I mean, it's really nice."

I thought Colt and Twila exchanged a glance across the table, but I might have imagined it. Nervous, I lifted my glass. The napkin stuck to the bottom. I took another drink, but the straw was too high. The raspy slurp of air on ice filled the kitchen. I felt like a mixed-breed Percheron at a tea party with purebred American Saddle Horses.

"Okay," Twila said, not lifting her gaze from me. "My ranch is really nice ... but ... ? But *what*? I want you to be honest with me, Scoop. What do you really think about our setup here?"

"No, I really mean it. It's good. It's a hundred times better than Dalton Stables." Who was I to say anything, good or bad, about her stables?

"Okay?" Twila said. Only her lips moved.

The rest of her sat motionless, staring at me. "Is it as nice for horses here as it is at Horsefeathers?"

"Well, Orphan wouldn't like it as much," I said. "But Horsefeathers and Cherokee Bend—they're like two different worlds. You give lessons here and camps. And you train and raise thoroughbreds. We only have a few horses, and most of them are backyard horses—like Orphan —horses their owners grew up with, in their backyards."

"Orphan?" Colt repeated.

I wheeled around to face him. "Yeah, Orphan," I said, as if he'd just made fun of my horse, which I won't put up with from anybody. "My mare."

Colt made a slight palms up gesture, signaling that he didn't mean anything by it.

Maybe he did and maybe he didn't.

"We don't *just* keep backyard horses," I went on. "Carla Buckingham keeps her show horse there, Ham." I didn't tell them Carla was one of my best friends. If it had been up to her parents, Ham never would have come to Horsefeathers in the first place.

"Buckinghams?" Colt said. "I know them. I showed against Carla when she rode Buckingham's British Pride last year. That's a fine horse. I came in second to it twice. *She* boards at Horsefeathers?" It felt like he was calling me a liar.

"*Ham*," I said as coolly as I could muster, "is Buckingham's British Pride."

"You're kidding," Colt said.

"Why wouldn't Orphan like it here as well as at Horsefeathers?" Twila only seemed to hear what she wanted to. I'd never met anybody like her.

"I didn't mean—I didn't even know there were *real* stables, commercial stables, this nice," I said, turning back to her.

She didn't say anything, but kept up that gaze. I gave up backpedaling. If she wanted to know, I'd tell her. "Okay," I said, resigned. "The way we're set up at Horsefeathers, our horses can be outside 24 hours a day if they feel like it. They could be inside all day too, if they wanted to. But I never met a horse who wouldn't rather be outside 90 percent of the time, especially if he can graze."

"But in the winter, don't you have to lock them in at night? If you leave the stall doors open, the horses will freeze inside the barn," Colt argued.

I didn't look at him, but kept talking to Twila, as if she'd been the one to ask. "Jen Zucker, my friend who helps out at Horsefeathers, she invented this latch that horses can nudge open when they want. And in the winter, the door will close up tight and keep the barn warm. Jen's brother Travis put the locks on all the stall doors. Every horse we've ever boarded has been able to learn how to open the stall door to come in or go out whenever they want."

"What else?" she asked.

I'd said this much. There wasn't much to lose by going on. "Where do your horses play?"

"Where do they play?" Colt asked it with a half-laugh.

"Yeah, play? I didn't see any balls or toys in the paddock. I'm guessing you have a pond in at least one of those pastures. But what about the others?"

"We've got electric water troughs in every stall," Colt said, as if I'd accused him personally.

Twila raised her hand, just an inch, but Colt stopped talking and leaned back in the booth, his fingers locked behind his head.

"We never have as many colts or broodmares at Horsefeathers as you do here," I said. "But if we did, I'd let all the colts and yearlings run together. They can learn a lot more about life and getting along with each other and us that way. Horses are horses' best teachers."

I stopped talking. What made me think I could tell them anything? I was nothing but the owner of one horse and keeper of a few others. Here she was, owner of who-knew-how-many prizewinning horses, running this huge operation, with someone like Colt as right-hand man.

"I'm sorry I went on like that—" I started.

At the opposite end of the kitchen, the glass rattled and someone tapped on the windowpane. They tapped again at least a dozen times.

Colt leaned forward, slapping both hands on the table. "Is it lesson time already?" he asked, craning around to see the tall grandfather clock in the corner. "Man!"

It was almost 5:00. I couldn't believe it either.

The tapping started again, and I looked across the kitchen to see two girls elbowing each other for position outside the window. They pressed their noses to the glass and waved—at Colt. They stood so close the pane fogged. The girls could have been sisters—blond, blue eyed, wearing the same English riding gear, jodhpurs, boots, button-down, short-sleeved shirt. One wore a riding hard hat, and the other one carried hers.

"Colt," Twila said, "I think your fan club's arrived."

6

Your fan club?" I repeated. Actually it didn't seem so far-fetched. Maggie 37 Brown had her own fan club, a group of middle-school boys mostly.

"They're not fans," he said. "Students." Twila stood, and Colt scooted out of the booth.

"You teach English riding lessons?" I asked, a little surprised that a ranch called Cherokee Bend would go in for English.

"He teaches all kinds of lessons, don't you, Colt?" Twila said.

"If you say so," he said. He turned to the window and gave the girls a smile and a wave, which seemed to send them into ecstasy. It made me think they would have been glad to take *math* lessons from Colt Cleveland.

He nodded at me. "See ya."

I nodded back, wondering if he would, see me.

"I'd better get you home before your aunt worries about you," Twila said, clearing the table. She dumped out the ice in a double steel sink, rinsed the glasses and put them in a dishwasher. She wiped off the near section of wood counters that ran all along two sides of the kitchen. Except for a hanging can opener, a toaster or breadmaker maybe, and a fancy napkin holder, the counters were clean as a whistle.

I followed her out the other side of the kitchen, through a sunny room filled with plants, past a cozy room with nothing in it except an easy chair and bookshelves filled with books. A narrow door opened to the garage, where a little red sporty car, a blue van, and a brown Jeep were parked.

The garage door lifted all by itself with a purr. Twila got behind the wheel of the Jeep, so I got in the other side. I'd never sat in a Jeep before, but I decided right then that if I ever owned transportation with wheels instead of hooves, it would be a Jeep.

She backed out of the garage without turning her head, then took off. Riding in the Jeep was like being outside or sitting on top of a car. The sky was our roof. Dust puffed up as we bounced down the dirt road. Twila's sunglasses must have kept the dust out of her eyes. I closed my eyes, then looked up at the setting sun as wind raced over every part of me.

It was almost too noisy to talk until we got near town and slowed down. The evening had turned cool enough to make me shiver, but I loved it.

Mr. Adams was out mowing his lawn, although it didn't need it. Two houses down, the Lowrys were planting flowers and pulling weeds. Mrs. Lowry still had on her real estate broker clothes.

We turned a corner, and it was the same scene. Lawn mowers drowned out the steady drone of crickets and birds. It got like this every spring, as if somebody sounded a huge gong and everybody sprang into action—mowing, watering, planting, weeding.

Everybody except us. Dotty didn't hear the gong.

"You'll have to tell me where you live, Scoop," Twila said.

"Turn up ahead," I said. But if I'd thought a minute I would have had her drop me off at Horsefeathers instead of at home.

We passed the Hat Lady's house—B.C.'s name for Dotty's friend who sits in front of us in church and wears huge hats every Sunday. She was wearing a broad-brimmed, straw hat today. The flower on top bounced as she crouched over her rose bushes. We were almost past her when she looked up just in time to see me.

I waved.

She waved, but looked shocked to see me in a Jeep.

We drove down Main Street. I was hoping somebody else would see me in this Jeep, but nobody paid us any attention. Then Travis and Jen Zucker walked out of the Hy-Klas, carrying groceries to Travis' pickup.

"Jen! Travis!" I yelled.

They looked up. Jen frowned through her glasses at us. Travis recognized me first. He grinned and waved back.

"That was Jen and Travis Zucker, the ones who figured out the locks for us at Horsefeathers," I explained. I thought about pointing out the Hy-Klas, where Dotty was probably checking and bagging groceries right now. But I didn't.

We were almost to my intersection. "You can just let me off here if you want," I said. "It was nice of you to drive me this far."

"Don't be silly, Scoop. Just tell me where to turn."

I told her to turn. We didn't say anything else as she crossed the railroad tracks. The houses got older. A handful had been abandoned. We bounced along our pot-holed road. Since nobody important lived on it, the town never bothered fixing the crumbled blacktop.

When Twila turned into our driveway, I got a weird feeling in my stomach. I'd known our yard needed mowing. I just hadn't realized how shaggy it had grown. We hadn't gotten around to borrowing Mr. Ford's lawnmower yet.

I'd have to move some of the stuff we'd ended up storing on the front lawn before we could mow. Dotty couldn't bear to throw anything away, especially appliances. At the end of the drive sat a washer I'd never seen anybody use. It had stayed there so long, I never noticed it anymore, until today.

Closer in was the stove Dotty refused to throw out "just because it doesn't work anymore." We'd gotten another one from Goodwill, but she held onto this one. Besides, it cost 10 dollars to have somebody come and haul a thing like that to the junk yard.

Nearer the house, other odds and ends had collected—a metal box, parts of wooden crates, the long handle of a farm tool that might have belonged to Grandad.

I sneaked a glance at Twila to see how she'd react to our house, which was about as different from hers as it could get. Our roof, patched with three different kinds of shingles, sagged in the middle as if an avalanche had fallen on it. The small, grayish house didn't look much different from the abandoned houses we'd passed. Everything hung crooked—the shutters, the window, the door, the porch.

But Twila didn't look down her nose at it. She stopped in the driveway, squinted toward the house, and turned to me. "Are you having a garage sale?" she asked.

For a minute her question threw me. We didn't even have a garage. Then I got it. It was because of all the junk on the lawn. She wasn't the first person to make that mistake. A couple of times, pure strangers had somehow stumbled across our road and our yard. The summer before, a young couple had knocked on our door and asked if the washing machine still worked.

Twila was smiling at me. She wasn't making fun or anything. Instead of saying *No. We're not having a garage sale. We're just hillbilly slobs who can't take care of their lawn,* I answered, "When we can get around to it."

Sorry, God, I prayed silently. *I promise I really will have a garage sale as soon as I can.*

I got out of the car and went around to the driver's side. "Thanks for everything," I said.

I glanced back at the house, expecting B.C. to run out at the sound of the car door and attack us when he saw the Jeep. He'd probably beg for a ride and ask Twila a thousand questions in two seconds flat. When I'd left him in the morning, B.C. had been watching Saturday morning cartoons. He was in the *manic* phase of his *manic depression*, which means he can talk faster than Alvin the Chipmunk.

But I didn't see B.C. I had to admit, I was glad.

"Thank *you*, Scoop," Twila said. She reached

into her tiny purse. "Here. I figure I owe you about—"

"No thank you," I said, stepping away from the Jeep so she couldn't give me the folded dollars. "I was just happy to see Lefty settled. I don't want anything for it."

I stopped talking. Twila's arm was frozen stiff, the money still in her fist. But she wasn't listening to me. She was staring up at something behind me. She was staring at the roof of our house, her eyes wide with fear.

Something plunked on her car and bounced with a pinging twang. *Ping, ping, ping.*

I knew without looking they were bottle caps. But Twila didn't seem to notice. She kept staring up.

And that's when I heard the screams. They were coming from the roof.

7

Ilooked back at the house, knowing what I'd see. B.C stood on top of the roof, a human chimney. But instead of spouting smoke, bottle caps erupted from him, arcing from the roof in a steady stream. About every second a bottle cap hit the hood of Twila's Jeep.

B.C.'s scream sounded like a siren, starting loud and then trailing low, as if he ran out of wind. Then it began again, full-pitched, and seeping out slowly.

"What—who is it?" Twila asked. She got out of the Jeep and I felt her behind me.

I had to forget about Twila Twopennies, forget what she would think of us, of me. This wasn't the first time my brother had thrown bottle caps off the roof. It wasn't even the first time he'd screamed his lungs out from that roof. But that didn't make it less scary. I couldn't know what he might do when he got like this.

"Scoop?"

I ignored Twila. I wished Dotty were home. Dotty would have a hundred times better chance of talking B.C. down than I would dragging him down. I ran toward the willow tree at the side of the house. I'd used it myself to get on the roof, where I do a lot of my best thinking and praying. The only drawback is that all the ants for miles around gather in that willow.

"Scoop, what can I do?"

"Go home!" I shouted. "I'm sorry. We'll be all right. I can handle this." *Lord*, I prayed, as I worked my way up the ant-filled willow tree, *I can't handle this. You're going to have to do it.*

I glanced down at the Jeep as I jumped to the roof. I could feel ants on my arms, and I slapped blindly at them.

Twila was standing by the Jeep, still not getting back inside, not driving away. I wanted her to leave. I wanted to forget I'd ever seen her or her ranch or her house or her limeade or her right-hand man.

B.C. stood in the exact center of the roof, as if he'd measured his position. He was wearing tan shorts that made me think of Boy Scouts and a #11 baseball jersey that the kid who owned it first probably loved wearing to Little League games his dad took him to. The shirt hung on little B.C.

"Stop screaming, okay?" I said. I didn't know if he'd seen me climb up, or if he even saw me now, when his eyes were aimed right at me.

But he must have heard me tell him to stop

screaming. He did the exact opposite, and started with another loud wail.

I waited him out, like sitting in church and waiting for the Hat Lady to run out of air and let go of the last high note so the song could be over and we could all go home.

B.C. ran out of air and collapsed, his knees flexing so he sat on his feet just in front of the chimney. His hair stuck out like an untrimmed hedge, autumn brown.

I made my way over to him and sat beside him. I put one arm lightly over his shoulder. He didn't pull away from me. His knees looked scuffed, and one of them was bleeding. He could have used a mom, a real mom who could fix knees and act surprised when he made her a card that said "Happy Mother's Day."

From below came the whispered question, "Scoop? Is everything okay?"

I couldn't see Twila until she backed up into our lawn, almost into the pile of would-be garage sale items. She waved and stood on her toes. "Can I do anything to help?"

I shook my head and hoped she could see it through the darkening dusk falling fast as bottle caps from a roof. I waved with my free hand, the one not on B.C.'s trembling shoulder. "Go on! Thanks!"

I was relieved to see her walk back to the Jeep. I heard the engine start, gravel spit. Then the Jeep backed slowly out of the drive and back where it came from, where it belonged, leaving us dust clouds that billowed and floated into the yard.

B.C. and I sat there as the night got colder and darker. I picked ants out of my hair and brushed them from my legs and arms.

"I hate her, I hate her, I hate her," B.C. said in a normal voice.

"Who, B.C.?" I asked.

He turned his big, brown eyes up at me, looking so much like a puppy somebody had kicked, I wanted to grab him and hold him. But I knew better. "I hate Grace Williams," he said.

A real mom would have known what to say about hating a girl named Grace Williams. Finally I asked, "How come you hate her, B.C.?" I thought I knew the kid—fourth grade like B.C., pretty.

B.C. breathed in deeply, and I thought he was going to cry. Instead, he screamed, louder and longer than before. When he ran out of air, I heard myself whistling. I kept whistling. It was "Amazing Grace." I can't carry a tune in a bucket, but I can whistle.

I figured B.C. would tell me about Grace, Grace Williams, not Amazing Grace, when he was good and ready. It was a safe bet that my brother really liked this girl instead of hated her. And I wouldn't have been surprised to find out

Tommy Zucker had his hand in this somehow.

Tommy is Jen and Travis' fourth-grade brother, one of the nine Zucker kids. Tommy's all right, but my brother is no match for him. When B.C. was still using his bottle caps to play army men, Tommy Zucker had established a profitable business venture selling his big sister's reports and homework.

Sitting on the roof, listening to cricket music and whispering leaves, I was just glad B.C. wasn't screaming anymore and that Dotty would be home any minute to help me get him off the roof.

I wondered how we'd look to Twila, or to Colt, as we sat in the sag of the roof in the dark. Which would have seemed weirder to them? A kid screaming and throwing bottle caps off the roof, or a skinny girl whistling "Amazing Grace" in the dark?

"Dotty," B.C. said, without looking up. I don't know how much time had passed.

We were still sitting cross-legged on the roof, so close our knees touched, and I didn't hear a thing for another 30 seconds. Sometimes I'm sure my brother hears things, and probably sees things, the rest of us don't.

First clue I heard was the brakes on the old Chevy. Then the crooked white beams of light turned into the drive. The headlights made uneven lines in the bushes beneath us.

The horn beeped once. I didn't know if she could see us up on the roof or not, but I waved. "Dotty! We're up here!"

B.C. watched, but didn't say anything.

Dotty wedged herself and one brown grocery bag out of the car. She still had on her orange Hy-Klas apron that fit too tight over uniform black pants. From our point of view looking down, she seemed shorter and squatter, her features blending together in the dark.

"Hey there!" she hollered, as cheery as if we'd greeted her with smiles and kisses at the front door of a happy home. "If it ain't my two favorite people on God's own earth!"

I waited for B.C. to make his move, to show us if it was over or not.

"You reckon we oughta get ourselves some supper?" she asked.

"You ready, B.C.?" I asked softly.

"Jesus," Dotty prayed, loud enough for all heaven to hear, "thank You for this beautiful night, for this here chocolate pudding I got on special down at the Hy-Klas. Come on down now." I was pretty sure the last part was meant for B.C. and me, although with Dotty I can never be sure. Her praying and talking are so mixed in together, it's hard to tell where the one leaves off and the other takes on.

B.C. stood up. With arms outstretched, he walked to the lowest sag part of the roof and jumped to the porch. I heard him land square and run three steps before the door slammed shut.

I could have done what B.C. did, jumped in the dark to the porch. Maybe it was being 15 now, five years older and wiser than B.C., that made me walk to the side and climb down the way I'd climbed up.

I'd forgotten about the willow tree ants until I was halfway down the tree. I jumped the rest of the way down, stomping and brushing and shaking off tiny black ants.

Something shiny caught my eye as I stepped to the porch. First moonlight washed over a small, sparkly lump next to the house. I walked up to it. Fifteen or 20 bottle caps were stacked neatly in even rows.

It was pretty nice of Twila, stacking up what had been thrown at her by a little kid she didn't even know. I picked up the bottle caps, wondering if any of them had flecks of brown paint on them, from where they'd scratched her Jeep.

I would probably never know. I'd never see Twila Twopennies again, or Cowboy Colt, or Lefty.

8

Our house had the familiar wet, musty smell it gets in spring, like a can of mushrooms left open. Our living room is about half as big as the Cherokee Bend kitchen. We'd had the couch as long as we'd had B.C., and I suppose my parents, Ben and Emma Coop, weren't the first to come by the gold, square couch that got darker with every year.

"Scoop?" Dotty called from the kitchen. "Wash your hands and come to supper." She went back to the sing-song of chatter she kept going to make up for the fact that B.C. wasn't talking.

I washed up and joined them in the kitchen, which smelled like the living room. The only time it smells like a kitchen is Thanksgiving or Christmas, or once in a great while when we stick in a roast before church on a Sunday.

Dotty had set out baloney slices on the white butcher's paper they'd come in. She set down a Styrofoam container, unopened, and stuck a spoon in a plastic tub of something that looked like three-bean salad.

B.C. sat at one of the unmatched chairs at the table, his elbows on the green-and-white plastic tablecloth, his chin in his hands.

"So Mr. Ford says to me—'Hey, Dotty,' he says, 'Dotty, that winder needs something.' I nods, like I know just what he's after. 'Dotty,' he says to me, and me with two customers waiting to be rung up. 'Dotty, see to that winder soon as you can.'"

I didn't listen to the whole story, but it ended with Dotty knocking down a pyramid of pork 'n' beans cans and us having pork 'n' beans out of a bent-up can.

"Lord," Dotty prayed, when she'd stopped laughing about the beans, "thank You for these two hearts here and for that bird singing on the way home, the one across from the schoolhouse, and for Miss Ella's back being so much better and her getting a letter from her son in California and don't let that young'un get into them drugs and all out there—"

I sneaked a peek at B.C. while Dotty was talking to God. He hadn't moved, hadn't closed his eyes.

"Amen. Pass them beans, will you?" Dotty held out her hands.

Since nobody else passed her the beans, I did.

Dotty chattered all during supper. B.C. didn't do more than bury his beans under his baloney. I got up to clear the table, and Dotty was putting lids back on uneaten supper, when my brother decided to talk.

"I don't hate Grace," he said, as if Dotty and I had just been insisting he did.

Dotty immediately stopped what she was doing and sat back down, scooting her chair as close as she dared to B.C. She didn't say anything, but waited, her square forehead wrinkled with listening.

"I love her," B.C. said. "But Tommy Zucker called up Grace on the telephone to ask her if she loved me back and she said she didn't—that she liked Tommy better." He said it all in one breath, like his scream, only low as a hum.

Dotty sighed, and her eyes glistened. She put her soft, fleshy arms around B.C., but he didn't seem to realize he was being hugged. He didn't move.

I didn't want this to turn into a crying fest. "B.C.," I said sternly, "did you ever stop to think that Tommy might not be telling the truth?"

He turned and frowned at me. The thought hadn't even occurred to him—or to Dotty, by the looks of her arched eyebrows that made her glasses move up on her nose.

"Duh!" I said. "Forget Tommy Zucker! You're tons cuter than he is, B.C. Go for it! Show this Grace girl that you've got a lot more to offer than sneaky Tommy Zucker."

"Scoop, now," Dotty said. "Ain't Tommy

one of B.C.'s buddies? You don't want to go saying bad things about him. Why can't the three of you be buddies? How about that, B.C.?"

But *I* still had B.C.'s attention.

"What do you mean about Tommy not telling the truth?" he asked me.

"Maybe Tommy just told you that Grace liked him because *he* likes *her*, B.C.," I said, plopping down beside him. "And anyway, so what if he does?"

"Tommy says he's going to ask Grace to go out with him," B.C. said.

"Go out where?" Dotty asked. "Why, his mama ain't going to let him take that little girl nowhere."

"He means go *out* with him," I explained. "They don't really go anywhere."

Dotty pushed herself up from the table. "Lord have mercy," she said. "Times is changed since I was a young'un." She shook her head and finished snapping the lids on supper.

"You just go to school on Monday, B.C., and act like nothing ever happened. I'll bet Tommy never even called Grace. Or if he did, he probably didn't even mention your name."

"B.C.?" Dotty said from the fridge. "You work on them spelling words for Monday?"

B.C. turned to her. "I can't, Dotty. They're too hard. One of them, I can't even say right. *Jog-free.*"

"It's *geography*," I said. "Here." I took out a pencil and wrote on the grocery bag. "George Ely's oldest girl rode a pig home yesterday."

Dotty shuffled over. "Diane Ely's girl?" she asked, astounded. "Nah!"

I laughed. "Not really. It's just the way I remembered how to spell geography." I underlined the first letter in each of the words. "See? It spells geography."

"George Ely's oldest girl rode a pig home yesterday!" B.C. repeated.

"You done got it!" Dotty exclaimed. "Scoop, will you give B.C. a hand with his arithmetic? I can't keep up no more."

"Dotty," I complained, "it's Saturday night!" I thought about Maggie, who probably had a date or two. And here I was at the kitchen table talking about riding pigs.

"I hate it when we leave homework to the last minute and B.C.'s got to do work on the Lord's day. It ain't right," Dotty said.

"All right," I said. "B.C., go get your bottle caps." For weeks, I'd been helping him with multiplication tables by using his bottle caps for counters. At least he didn't fuss as much. If we had a mother, a real mother, she could be doing this instead of me.

The phone rang.

"I'll get it," Dotty said. "Might be the pastor wanting me to do child care for church. I know

Lucille's been sickly."

I listened to Dotty's end of the conversation. "Who's this now? Twila What?"

I dashed to the living room and pulled the phone out of Dotty's hands. "I got it," I said.

I cleared my throat. "Hello?"

"Scoop?" said the soft, almost musical voice that seemed to be seeping through the phone from another world. "This is Twila Twopennies."

I listened, not daring to speak. When she stopped, I held my hand over the phone receiver, stretched the cord as far as it would pull, and whispered into the kitchen at Dotty. "Twila Twopennies wants to know if it's okay for me to help her at her stables!"

"Who's Twila Two—?" Dotty asked, too loud.

"She's nice," I said, so nervous my stomach felt like horses were trotting through it. "I was there today. It's okay, Dotty. I really want to go help!"

"Well, that's fine then," she said, wiping her hands on a dish towel. "When?"

I heard something through the phone. Afraid Twila had hung up, I whipped the receiver back to my ear so fast the phone bonked my head. "I'm sorry, Twila," I said into the phone. "Are you there?"

"Yes."

"When did you want me to come to Chero-kee Bend?" I asked.

"I could pick you up at about 9:00 tomorrow. I need you for the day."

"Great!" I said. "Just a minute."

I covered the receiver again. "Dotty, she'll come get me at nine tomorrow."

"Tomorrow? Scoop, did you forget tomorrow is Sunday?" Dotty asked.

I *had* forgotten. "It's just this one time, Dotty. I want to go so much!"

Dotty shook her head. "That's fine, but not on the Lord's day. You can go another time."

"Please! I'll get up early and read my Bible on my own and pray and sing if you want me to!" My stomach knotted. It felt like if I said no to Twila, I was saying no to a whole lot more than just going out there on Sunday.

"Scoop," Dotty said, "we made us a promise to God to worship Him in church on Sunday. You can go after church. How about that?"

I sighed and cleared my throat before going back to the phone. "Um, would it work out if I came in the afternoon?"

"Oh." Twila sounded disappointed. "I'm afraid it won't. Are you sure you can't work it out for the morning?"

I couldn't stand it. What would it hurt to miss one Sunday? One glance at Dotty told me she wasn't going to change her mind. "I'm afraid not," I said weakly, my throat closing off.

"Well ... all right. Thanks anyway, Scoop. Good-bye." After a second of silence, the phone clicked as softly as the swish of a horse's tail.

It might not have been right, but I was so mad at Dotty after I hung up the phone, I couldn't even talk to her. This wasn't fair. Dotty wasn't my mother. What gave her the right to keep me from going where I wanted to—where I really wanted to go?

"Scoop?" Dotty called from the kitchen as I climbed the stairs to my bedroom. "Don't forget B.C.'s arithmetic. He's waiting here with his bottle caps. You coming?"

Dotty didn't wait for an answer. It wasn't really a question. I trudged back to the kitchen and started plunking down metal bottle caps in groups of four. I was relieved when Dotty left the kitchen and I heard the bath water running. If she'd said one word to me, she'd have been sorry. We'd both have been sorry.

Instead, I heard her whistling "Amazing Grace" as the water trickled into the bathtub.

B.C. tried to understand how four groups of four bottle caps was the same as four times four. But I couldn't concentrate on his math problems. I had problems of my own. I wondered if that was the last time I'd ever hear from Twila Twopennies. And I wondered why I cared so much.

Crickets were chirping, and the sun sparkled on beads of dew as Dotty, B.C. and I headed out on foot for church. I'd only said about 10 words to Dotty since Twila's call, but I don't think she'd noticed. She was too busy trying to bring B.C. around.

Dotty inhaled the chilly air. "I can almost taste spring!" she declared. Although B.C. and I were walking regular speed, and Dotty was staying even with us, she seemed to be scurrying. "B.C.," she said, like she was asking his advice on an important business investment, "you tell me how many shades of green you see here."

B.C. shrugged.

"I betcha them greens on that there budding tree is more shades than you gotcha bottle caps," she said. "Our heavenly Father sure outdone Hisself with different colors of green! You reckon green is His favorite color?"

"There's Jen!" I said, distancing myself from B.C. and Dotty when we got close to church.

Jen and Travis Zucker met me on the steps.

Jen looked pale and thin, but healthy enough. Maggie says Jen is fine-boned anyway and naturally pale. Her wispy blond hair fell to her shoulders. Wire-rimmed glasses look better on Jen than they do on anybody I've ever seen. She has a kidney disease, but she's fighting it. Her whole family is fighting with her—all nine kids and two real parents.

"Hey, Jen! Hey Travis," I said, resisting the urge to ask Jen how she felt. That drives her crazy. *Kidney disease doesn't just go away and you wake up well*, she'd told me a couple of weeks earlier when I'd ask how she felt. *I'll let you know when there's a change. Until then, treat me like a normal person.*

It wasn't easy. Jen Zucker had never been a normal person—any more than her horse, Cheyenne, was a normal horse.

"So where were you, Scoop?" Jen asked.

"What?" Something nagged at the back of my mind.

"Maggie thought you might not have gotten back from Cherokee Bend in time. But I thought you'd at least call."

Then I remembered. "Horsefeathers!" Our Saturday night meeting. I'd forgotten all about it. "I'm sorry, Jen! I forgot. And I did get back kind of late anyway." I thought back. While they were meeting, I was probably sitting on the roof with my brother.

Travis elbowed me. "So what's she like? Twila Twopennies. I've never seen her. Maggie said she looks exactly like you, only older."

"She's nice," I said. Travis is so handsome, sometimes I can't get a lot of words to come out when I look at his big, blue eyes.

"And ... ?" he urged.

"And she's much prettier than I am."

He smiled, and I wondered how I ever could have thought any guy, even Colt, was as good looking as Travis.

"Prettier than you?" Travis teased. "I can't even imagine that, Scoop." He waved at somebody inside the church and trotted on in. Dotty and B.C. moved past us up the stairs.

"What did you do at the Horsefeathers meeting, Jen?" I asked. "Were Carla and Maggie there too?"

"Yes. We spent the whole time discussing the parade," Jen said, moving toward the entry.

"What parade?" I asked.

Jen frowned at me. "Maggie said you knew about it. The Mother's Day parade. We decided to involve the whole town. Maggie is really gung-ho on this. I believe we should get quite a bit of publicity."

"I don't want to be in a Mother's Day parade," I whined.

Jen seemed surprised. "But I thought you and Maggie were in on this together. Horsefeathers horses will lead the parade. Maggie's contacting churches and clubs. Carla is writing something for the newspaper. You *own* the stable, Scoop. You *have* to be in the parade."

We took the stairs to the basement, where our Sunday school class met. The room smelled dank, and the only other ninth graders were Carla and Ray and Megan.

"Scoop!" Carla called from across the room. Her folding chair was as close to Ray's as it could get. She waved at us to sit by them.

Ray nodded as I took the seat on the other side of Carla. Jen sat next to me and started talking to Megan.

"Maggie says you have a look-alike out there. Say it isn't so, Scoop," Ray said, in the easygoing way that makes him easy to talk to. If he were a horse, he'd be a lanky Tennessee Walking Horse.

Ray and I had been friends for over 10 years before Carla moved to West Salem. Ray and I are still friends, but he and Carla are more than that. Sometimes it's fine being around them, and sometimes I feel like the third horse in a two-horse trailer.

"I don't know why Maggie says Twila looks like me," I said, tugging on my braid. I'd tried braiding it tighter, in one braid down the middle of my back. But I knew it wasn't neat like Twila's braid.

"So this isn't some long-lost relative come to claim you?" Ray said, teasing like he always does.

"You wish," I said. *I wish*, was more like it.

"We missed you at the meeting," Carla said. It sounded like *We miss you add mee-ing*. Carla is hearing impaired, but you'd never know it to look at her. She's beautiful, and her long, shiny hair hides her hearing aids. I used to have trouble understanding her, but I never do anymore. "I rode Ham before we met, and he moved great," Carla continued. "Got his leads every time. He'll be ready for the parade."

I was glad Mr. and Mrs. Cellars started class and I didn't have to talk to Carla about the stupid parade. All during Sunday school my mind kept wandering to Cherokee Bend. I couldn't help imagining what I would have been doing if Dotty hadn't been so stubborn. Maybe Twila was going to have me work with Lefty or Dream. Maybe I would have been working with Colt.

I'd never know, thanks to Dotty.

When I tuned back in to our Sunday school teacher, even he was talking about the parade. "I expect your class to help out with our church float. If you have an idea for it, talk to Mrs. Powers."

After Sunday school, I hurried up the steps before Carla could ask me about the Mother's Day parade. I plopped down in the pew next to B.C.

A minute later Dotty scooted in next to me.

I had thought she'd be downstairs with the nursery. Mrs. Powers, the Hat Lady, turned around when Dotty sat down. Today her hat was green with a yellow flower tucked into a darker green band. Where Dotty was short and thick, the Hat Lady was tall and slim—an American Saddle Horse to Dotty's Shetland Pony.

"Dotty," she said, "did you hear about the parade?"

Great. I couldn't get away from Maggie's monster parade no matter what I did.

"What parade is that?" Dotty asked. Tiny beads of sweat formed above her upper lip. She tugged at the hem of her blue-and-white polka dot dress, the one she wore almost every Sunday.

"Didn't you hear? The town is putting on a Mother's Day Parade the Saturday before Mother's Day. Isn't that a lovely idea?" The Hat Lady smoothed part of her white hair back. Then she reached over and patted my brother's arm.

B.C. looked up from the bulletin and grinned back at her.

"That's a great idea!" Dotty said. "There ain't no better job God gives a body than to be a mother."

"Our lady's group is in charge of making a float. I said you'd help. You will, won't you, Dotty?" Mrs. Powers glanced at the organist when she started up.

"I sure enough will!" Dotty declared.

Thankfully we all had to rise and sing.

Pastor Dan talked from Romans 8. When he read verse 23 about all of us groaning for adoption as God's children, I started thinking about it. I'd been adopted. I'd always known that. But what did I know about my real parents? Nothing. What if they decided to come and find me one day? I'd thought about it before, but it had always been more of a game, a what-if dream. I'd missed my adoptive parents so much, I hadn't had room to miss the parents I was born to.

After church I walked outside with Jen and Travis. A Baltimore oriole sat on the hickory in front of church. It sang, and with each note, its tail twitched. Behind the chirping were the sounds of crickets here and there.

"Jen," I said, suddenly remembering the summer when crickets had come out of the ground and chirped for weeks. "Remember those crickets that almost drove us crazy that summer? What were they called?" I knew she'd know.

"Cicada," she answered. "But you don't have to worry about them for another 17 years. They only come out every 17 years to make babies. Then they go back underground."

I walked home by myself. What if my real mom was like the cicada? What if she'd given birth to me and planned to come back for me later—maybe 17 years, or maybe just about 15½?

10

The week dragged on. Maggie seemed to be as obsessed about Twila as I was. I told her what Colt had said about Twila running off on graduation night. I had a twang of guilt for passing along gossip, but Maggie thought it was wonderful and romantic.

I found myself sitting by the phone, wondering, hoping, praying Twila would call. B.C. had a new Grace drama every afternoon, like a soap opera, with Tommy Zucker as the villain. Most of the dramas ended with B.C. crying on the roof.

At school all activity centered on Mother's Day and Maggie's parade. In art we were doing cut-outs on squares of linoleum—so we could make Mother's Day cards to give our mothers. In history class we were supposed to draw a tree, a genealogical study of our maternal ancestry. In fifth grade when we'd had to make a family tree report, I'd made mine up and gotten in trouble.

Tuesday night I sat at the kitchen table drawing empty leaves on my family tree. "Dotty," I said, slamming down my pencil, "don't you know *anything* about my family?"

Dotty was perched on a stool, hunched over a wastebasket as she tried to make flowers out of pink Kleenex, her assignment for the church's Mother's Day float. "I reckon I do know a mite bit," she said.

I turned to face her. I'd always been told nobody had any real information on my biological parents. "What, Dotty? Tell me!"

"Well, I reckon you know about the Coops from your granddaddy—God rest his soul. Emma's daddy came—"

"Not them!" I said, disappointment as hot as lava flowing through me. "My *real* parents, Dotty. My *real* family."

Dotty glanced over at me, her eyes shiny like when she peels onions on that stool. "Well, I'm sorry, Scoop. I reckon I always thought of Emma and Ben Coop as your real family."

"Dotty," I said, sounding sorrier than I felt at the moment, "you know what I mean. I mean my biological family." I didn't want to hurt her feelings. "It's for school," I said.

"Emma never talked about that," Dotty said. "I don't rightly think she knew more than she let on though. You was in foster care so long and all."

"I was what?" I asked. "What do you mean I was in foster care so long?"

Dotty put down her deformed Kleenex flower and stared at me. "I thought you knew that. You was 3 when Emma adopted you."

"I do know that, Dotty," I said. "It's just ... well, I thought I'd been with my mother, I mean my biological mother, until then."

"My no!" Dotty exclaimed. "There ain't a mama on earth could have had you three years and let go! You was such a precious thing."

I'd never come right out and admitted it to myself, but it had hurt to believe that my mother had kept me for three years and then decided she didn't want me. I used to wonder if I might have done something so rotten she couldn't stand more than three years of me. "Then who had me for three years?" I tried not to look as desperate as I was starting to feel. Part of me felt trapped somewhere back before I was 3. I had to go back and find myself before it was too late.

"I reckon you wasn't born out of state or nothin'," Dotty said. "By the time Emma done heard about you, you was in more homes than you could shake a stick at. You was in foster care from the day you left the hospital. That did it for your mama. Emma knew right away you was the child for her and Ben."

So my mother hadn't rejected *me*, not really *me*. She'd given up a baby she didn't know. I stared quickly down at my barren genealogical tree, and a fat tear plopped right where a leaf should have been. "I'll finish this later," I said, scraping my chair back and hurrying upstairs to my bedroom.

I thought about it for hours before I fell asleep that night. A lot of weird memory flashes made sense now. The reason I couldn't remember those first three years was that every time I tried to picture my *mother* or home, a different face or room slid by me. No wonder! Who knows how many places I'd been in those three years!

But what about my real mother? What if she did surface, like the cicada, to try to find her daughter? What chance would she have of trailing me through foster parents and adoptive parents who were dead?

The rest of the week, I felt like I was only half there, going through the motions of classes and homework and chores. The only thing that kept me sane was taking Orphan out every afternoon to our favorite spot deep in the woods or out on country back roads. I slipped back into my old ways of imagining I was an Indian princess. Only when I closed my eyes, I looked more and more like Twila Twopennies.

I missed Lefty too. I knew she would be fine at Cherokee Bend, but I still felt like I could burst into tears every time I thought of her.

Friday at lunch I sat down at an empty table. Maggie, dressed in green from the collar of her short dress to her green ballet shoes, joined me, and instantly the table filled.

"Scoop, my dear," said Maggie 37 Green in what could probably pass as a Scottish accent. "Have ye been a-hearing the gr-r-rand plans of our par-r-rade now? Not just your own church, but all the town's churches are partaking in the festivities. Even the football team is putting together a float that says, 'We get a *kick* out of mothers!' And on the other side, 'Our *goal* is to be like Mom!'"

"You know how I feel about this Mother's Day parade, Maggie," I said. But I knew she didn't know how I felt. Nobody did.

Jen set down her tray and opened a huge book. She usually reads at lunch, although I can't imagine reading in all the cafeteria commotion.

"Scoop," Maggie said, one eye on Jen, "when are you going to Cherokee Bend again?"

"Probably never," I said, "if it's up to Dotty."

I thought I saw Jen and Maggie exchange secret glances. "What?" I asked.

"Maggie," Jen said, scolding like she might have warned Tommy.

Maggie ignored her. "Scoop, what do you really know about Twila Twopennies? I think you should ask her straight out if she had a baby like Colt said she did. You should just—"

"Maggie!" Jen snapped. "I told you not to—"

"What is this?" I asked. "Have you two been talking behind my back?"

Carla walked up and stood behind Jen. "Did you ask her how old Twila is or when she had the baby?" Carla grinned defensively when Jen wheeled around to frown at her. "I was reading your lips, okay?"

"Stop it, you two!" Jen said, frowning from Maggie to Carla. "You call this subtle?"

"What's going on?" I asked.

Maggie leaned in closer to me. "Don't tell me you're not the least bit curious why Twila Twopennies looks exactly like you, loves horses like you do, maybe had a baby she gave up for adoption?"

I started chewing my fingernails. Something twisted in my stomach, and I knew I couldn't eat. "Wha-what are you saying?" I demanded. The clang of forks thrown into metal bins grew deafening, punctuated by bursts of laughter.

Carla glanced at Maggie. Maggie looked at Jen. Then Maggie said, "I'm just saying you should *think* about it, Scoop. I mean, if Twila really did have a baby and gave it up for adoption, maybe. ... "

"Maggie!" I said. I knew where she was going with this. I should have laughed at the very idea of it—Twila Twopennies, *my* mother? It was ridiculous.

But something about the idea didn't feel

ridiculous, didn't even come as a surprise. The one potato chip I'd eaten turned to a brick in my stomach.

Jen stared at me, her eyes filled with pity. "Now look what you've done," she whispered.

But the door to my mind was open. Thoughts blew in and out, and I couldn't stop them. *Twila Twopennies. Adoption. Mother's Day.* I wanted to find the nearest roof and climb it.

"I told you, Maggie!" Jen said. "None of this is logical," she insisted. "The odds are infinitesimal."

"Sorry, Scoop," Carla said, but her voice seemed to come from outer space.

My mind was swirling. Thoughts soared, came closer, fluttered, then flew off, like flocks of birds refusing to light.

Maggie put one arm around my shoulder. "Well I'm not sorry. Scoop, you have to face it. You have to find out."

"Maggie!" Jen whispered sharply.

I shook off Maggie's arm. "Find out? That's crazy." But in my heart I'd already bumped against every single idea Maggie could have had about Twila Twopennies. I just hadn't dared let the thoughts sink into my soul.

What if Twila Twopennies really was—but that was crazy, like imagining I was an Indian princess.

I pushed away from the table, spilling my

milk. Thin white liquid seeped into my hamburger bun. "I'm not hungry," I mumbled, leaving my tray, leaving my friends.

"Scoop!"

I heard them calling me, but I didn't turn around.

I hurried out of the cafeteria. My shoulder rammed into somebody.

"Hey! Watch where you're going!" It was Stephen Dalton. "Scoop," he said, "are you okay? You look funny." Even *he* sounded like he felt sorry for me.

Thankful I had study hall next, I eased into the library and found a seat by myself in the back by the window. My cheeks were wet with tears I couldn't remember crying. I sensed the sideways glances of several kids, but it felt like they were on a different planet.

What *did* I know about Twila Twopennies? Not very much.

Over the years, I had imagined a lot of different mothers—everyone from Princess Di to my first grade teacher. But this was different, more real. What was it about Twila Twopennies that made me think that maybe, possibly, she might be my real mother?

I tried to remember every word she'd said. I racked my brain to come up with anything, any sign that maybe she was trying to tell me herself. But there was no sign.

Maybe, I thought, as the bell rang and I walked zombie-like through the rest of my classes, maybe Twila didn't know who I was. When I was born, the details of adoptions were kept secret, even from the birth mothers.

I pictured her as I'd seen her last, from my spot on the roof, as she backed out the Jeep and drove away. Something about her leaving had been so sad, but so expected, as if that hadn't been the first time I'd watched her drive away. The more I envisioned it, going over every little detail, the more sure I was. It had happened before. Something about being dropped off by Twila Twopennies had felt as familiar as ... as ... as familiar as limeade.

11

"S coop! You're not paying attention!"
Friday night B.C. and I were bent over piles
of bottle caps on the kitchen table. He was right.
I wasn't paying attention. "I hate math! I don't
get it!" he cried.

"Sorry, B.C.," I said. "It's 27. Remember?
Count them—nine piles of three each."

"No," B.C. whined. "That was when we had
only three piles and nine bottle caps in each one!
Why are you smart, like Tommy and Grace, and
I'm stupid?"

"B.C.," I said, brushing his hair out of his
eyes, "you are the smartest, sweetest brother
God ever gave—"

Dotty pushed through the front door, her
arms weighed down with white plastic bags full
of Hy-Klas specials-of-the-day or out-of-date deli
items.

"Dotty!" B.C. yelled, as if she'd been gone
for months instead of hours.

"How's my handsome boy?" she asked.
"And strong! Will you look at that! You can't

hardly carry all them bags, can you, B.C.?"

"I can too!" B.C. said, grunting his way into the kitchen, dragging the bags. "Do you think I'm as strong as Tommy Zucker?" asked B.C. He hoisted the bags onto the counter. "Grace sat with Tommy at lunch today. I sat by myself, but I ate really fast and went outside for recess."

I raked B.C.'s bottle caps back into his shoebox. Dotty hugged my shoulders from behind. "How was your day, Honey?" she asked.

"Fine," I said, leaving out the part about how Maggie was almost positive that Twila Twopennies was my real mother. But since Dotty had ruined what might have been my only chance of finding out for sure, I'd never know. And all because Dotty didn't want me to miss church one single Sunday.

It took all the willpower I had to keep my cool. "Dotty, do you think my mother ... my birth mother, I mean ... came from around here?"

"Why do you care all of a sudden?" B.C. asked, standing close to Dotty. Them against me.

Dotty shuffled over to the table and sat down. I acted like I was studying B.C.'s bottle caps. "I don't know about that, Scoop," she said. "I reckon you was born in the state all right. Adoptions is easier in the same state."

"So what?" B.C. demanded. "Who cares? You were born with me! Here! I remember!"

"Was it somebody they knew?" I asked.

"No, I'm sure not," Dotty said, finger-combing B.C.'s hair. "I don't know how it happened exactly, but I reckon the good Lord had His plan fixed all along to bring you to your mama. You was the cutest thing I ever seen."

"But do you know what adoption agency they went through?" I asked. I'd given up trying to act like it didn't matter. It did. It mattered more every minute.

Dotty shook her head. "Your mama always thought some couple was just too young to bring you up and they loved you enough to give you up," Dotty said.

B.C. shoved between Dotty and me. "Stop it! I don't like this. Don't talk anymore!"

I got up. Dotty didn't know anything more anyway. But she'd given me a piece of the puzzle. The leaves on my barren genealogical tree were budding.

"B.C., Honey," Dotty said, her voice cheery. "Guess what us ladies at the church is calling our float." She glanced at me. "Scoop?"

We didn't guess, so she told us. "'Hats off to mothers!' Ain't that good!"

"Did you think of it yourself?" B.C. asked.

"Nope," Dotty said. "Can you reckon who done thought of it though?"

"The Hat Lady!" B.C. shouted.

"Ain't you smart, B.C.!" Dotty declared.

"But you don't have a hat," B.C. said, his mood changing as suddenly as a wind storm.

"Don't you worry none about that," Dotty said. "You ain't gotta have a hat to stuff them Kleenex into them chicken wire holes. 'Sides, if I rode on one of them floats, I'd probably fall off."

But B.C. didn't like that answer. "No!" he said, loud as thunder. "They should let you ride on the float! I want you to ride on it!"

Dotty didn't miss a beat. "Lord, B.C. here wants me to ride that there church float. You heard him, I reckon. So, if You agree with him, then I guess You gotta find me a hat."

"Prettier than the Hat Lady's hat!" B.C. yelled. I didn't know if he was yelling it to God or us.

The phone rang.

"I'll get it!" I jumped up so fast I bumped the table. The shoebox tipped, and bottle caps rained onto the linoleum behind me as I raced to the living room.

"Scoop!" B.C. yelled. "My bottle caps!"

I caught the phone on the second ring. "Hello?" My voice cracked, so I said it again. "Hello."

"Scoop?" It was really her! Twila Twopennies! I recognized her voice as if I'd been hearing it my whole life. "Is that you?"

"Yes," I said, my heart beating so fast I didn't trust myself to say another word. I knew she'd call. I knew it.

"Twila Twopennies here."

As if I didn't know.

"I was wondering if you might be available to work for me tomorrow. Colt will be tied up with Saturday lessons, and some of the brood-mares need extra attention."

"Yes!" I said. "I'd love to come."

"I apologize for the late notice. Colt had someone else lined up, but he backed out at the last minute." She sounded so official, so business-like. If she was my mother—and that was still a giant *if*, I reminded myself—she probably had no idea.

"When do you need me? When do you want me to come?" I managed to ask. "I can come anytime."

"Fine. 9:00 then? I'll come by your house and pick you up."

"Wait!" I glanced into the kitchen and saw that both B.C. and Dotty were listening to every word I said. I turned my back to them and said, "Um ... Would you mind just picking me up at Horsefeathers?" I didn't want to risk B.C. on the roof again. I didn't want Twila to meet Dotty or ask her when we were having our garage sale.

"That's fine," she said, and she listened while I gave her directions.

I'd started to hang up when I heard her say, "Scoop?"

I whipped the phone up, smashing my ear this time. "Yes? I'm here."

"If you'd like to bring your horse, that would be fine too. We may need to ride back in the pastures to check on some of the stock."

I stood there, clutching the phone long after I heard the soft click on the other end, just to make sure she wasn't still on the line. My fingers didn't want to let go.

I hung up and immediately dialed Maggie. Miraculously, she was home. She hadn't finished hello before I was pouring out everything—all about the fosters and in-state adoptions and Twila's phone call and my own gut feelings—the dandelions, limeade, everything.

"Scoop," Maggie said softly, and I realized that I'd never talked more and she'd never talked less. "Deep in your heart of hearts, what do you really think?"

We were so quiet I could hear Maggie's parents laughing at a TV show in the background. "Maggie," I said at last, "I think ... I think Twila Twopennies is my real mother."

12

Saturday morning I was up and on my way to Horsefeathers before the sun even thought about getting up. A thick fog hugged the ground so I couldn't see more than a horse's length in front of me. It still sounded like night, with crickets sending steady buzzes in waves. I might have been hiking in an all-new world. That's what it felt like.

I hadn't slept much the night before. For hours I'd lain in bed imagining what it would be like to live with my real mother. Thinking of anyone as my *real* mother still made me feel like a traitor. Emma Coop had been my real mother. She'd adopted me and raised me the best she could till the day she died. Nothing would ever change that. But I thought she'd understand. Maggie said she would.

Turning up Horsefeathers Lane, I could smell horses and the barn, but I still couldn't see them. I crossed to the back pasture where I figured Orphan, Moby, and Cheyenne had spent the night close to the pond.

White fog lay over the pastures like a cloud, as if the sky had fallen, but caught itself just in time. I could almost feel God as I prayed: *Thank You, Lord, for bringing Twila back. Thanks for the revelations today will bring to both of us.*

I whistled for Orphan. From somewhere deep in the pasture she answered with a long whinny. I heard thundering hooves, but couldn't see her. I got the feeling that God was lifting earth up, with me on it, bringing us up as far as heaven's basement.

The hoofbeats got louder. Orphan burst through the fog as if dropping from a cloud, sneaking back from heaven-side to be with me. At a full gallop, she raced out of clouds, her black mane and tail flying in the morning breeze. She skidded to a stop in front of me, and I threw my arms around her neck. Her black coat smelled like dew.

"Come on, Girl," I whispered, rubbing behind her ears. "Today we just may be going to my mother's." It felt strange to say it out loud, like I was giving in, like when B.C. stopped fighting himself and admitted that he loved Grace.

By the time the sun finally came up, I had Orphan dry-washed, brushed, shined, and ready to go, all under the watchful eye of the purring barn cat, Dogless. I polished Orphan's halter and bridle, grained all the horses, groomed them, and cleaned their hooves.

I'd worn my best blue jeans, newest boots, a red shirt that fit me well and Maggie said flattered my figure. We'd selected it over the phone. I'd even used hairspray on the tight braid that hung down my back. But I still had to muck the stalls.

I had pitchfork in hand when I heard a car drive up. Panic grabbed at my throat. Horsefeathers! She was early! I hadn't finished chores. I still had to throw hay to the loft. I wanted to sweep up before she saw the stables, straighten the HORSEFEATHERS sign out front.

A car door slammed. Then another one. I ran outside. Carla and Ray, in matching grubbies, hopped out of the back of Travis' beat-up, white pickup.

"Herr Scoop?" Ray called, saluting. "We have come as commanded! We report for duty!"

"Leave the accents to Maggie 37, Ray," Carla said, laughing.

Jen, Maggie, and Travis piled out of the cab. Dogless zipped around me and pranced out to meet Travis, the cat's favorite human.

"We would have been here earlier if certain people didn't take so long to get glamorous," Travis said, grinning over at Maggie.

Maggie did look beautiful. Her hair fell around her shoulders in a couple of dozen dreadlocks, and she was obviously Maggie 37 Red today, in red jeans, red checkered shirt, and red boots. "I will take that as a compliment, Herr Zucker," she said, in a much better German accent than Ray's. "But do not expect such flattery will get you out of the dirtier jobs here."

Ray yawned and tilted his head to rest on Carla's shoulder. I was pretty sure Ray normally slept until noon on Saturdays. Only Carla could have gotten him to come this early.

"Thanks for coming, everybody," I said. "I forgot we were doing this today."

"You mean I got up this early for nothing?" Ray said, without opening his eyes or moving his head from Carla's shoulder.

"Nothing?" Carla said. "You call spending a few extra hours with me, *nothing*?"

"Scoop," Jen said, her hands on her hips, "how could you forget? The parade is a week from today! With any luck, a lot of people will come by to check out Horsefeathers." Jen was wearing a jacket and a sweatshirt, and she was still shivering. "I know you hate Mother's Day, but this parade will be great publicity for us—*if* Horsefeathers looks its best."

I felt bad that I'd forgotten, that I'd missed our last meeting. But none of it seemed to matter anymore. It was like they were still in a world I'd floated out of. "Sorry," I said. "You guys are great to come help." I kicked at the dirt and didn't look at any of them. "I'm really sorry I can't stay and help too."

Ray's eyes opened wide. "You're kidding, right?"

Maggie rushed to my defense. "No problem! We can handle Horsefeathers. Scoop can't stay because she has vital work to do today. Life-changing work." She winked at me, and I felt my face burn.

Jen rolled her eyes. She saw through Maggie's little speech.

Travis walked all the way around me, like he was sizing up a horse at auction. "Hmmm," he said. "Vital, life-changing work, huh? You do look mighty glamorous yourself, Scoop. Do you have a big date you're not telling us about?"

I figured my face was probably as red as my shirt. "I told Twila Twopennies I'd give her a hand at her ranch today."

"Maggie," Jen said, "is this your idea?"

"No!" Maggie said, her lips pouty. "It was Twila's idea. So there! What do you think about *that?*" Maggie folded her arms in front of her defiantly. I suspected this argument had been going on for days.

"What do I think?" Jen asked calmly. "I think Twila Twopennies knows a great horse whisperer when she sees one. *And* I think that you're getting Scoop's hopes up when it's probably just a coincidence."

"What's a coincidence?" Travis asked, squinting from Jen to me. "Am I the only one missing something here?"

One glance at Ray told me he knew what was going on. Travis *was* the only one in the dark.

Maggie obviously wanted another ally. "Travis," she said, getting eye-to-eye with him, "Twila Twopennies looks exactly like Scoop—I told you that. They like all the same weird things. We think Twila had a baby when she was really young and that she gave it up for adoption. And—"

"Wait a minute," Travis interrupted. He glanced at me, then back at Maggie. "If you're saying what I think you're saying, that's a huge leap."

"Exactly," Jen said.

"Scoop?" Travis stared at me until I had to look him in his big, concerned blue eyes. "Do you really think Twila Twopennies is your birth mother?"

I couldn't bring myself to answer him.

"Because she looks like you?" Travis said gently. "Because she likes horses and *maybe* had a baby?"

When he said it like that, he made it sound farfetched. I could feel my hope melt like a sugar cube in water, dissolving a grain at a time.

"Okay, okay," Maggie said. "We didn't say we were sure. We just said she *might* be Scoop's mother."

More than anything, I wanted them all to leave me alone. The fog in my head was as thick as the fog gathered around us. Maybe Travis and Jen were right. So she looked like me and liked limeade. So what? Maybe Twila was no more my mother than I was an Indian princess.

Maggie put her arm around my shoulder. "Scoop, you *have* to ask her. You may never get another chance."

"Right, Maggie," I said. "What exactly should I ask? 'Twila, by the way, did you give birth to me 15 or so years ago?'"

"That's how I'd handle it," Travis said, his white teeth gleaming as he stroked the cat. I knew he was trying to let me off the hook, to lighten the situation with humor.

But Maggie wouldn't be put off. "Of course not!" she said. "Ask her about her marriage— what year they got married, why they broke up, if she's ever had a baby."

Carla came to my rescue and ordered everybody to start cleaning. Ray and Carla would throw the hay to the loft, and Jen and Maggie would stack bales. Travis and I started in on the stalls.

"Scoop," he said, shoveling out old straw and manure, "does it bother you that you were adopted?"

"Would it bother you?" I asked, matching him load for load, both of us pitching the manure into a wheel barrow.

"Probably," he said.

I was thinking out loud as much as talking to Travis. "It's like part of me is angry that anybody would just give me away. Sometimes it feels like I'm adopted because I wasn't good enough to be a regular daughter." I stabbed the manure and straw harder and didn't look at Travis.

"There you're wrong, Scoop," he said softly. "Remember what Pastor Dan read about all of us being adopted by God? It's not a secondhand way to slip into a family. Jesus had to die and be raised from the dead so we could have our sins forgiven and become part of *His* family. Adoption is a big deal, a good thing, like God took extra planning to—"

"She's here!" Maggie screamed. "She's pulling a black trailer like last time!"

I dropped the pitchfork and ran out of the stall. Twila's truck and empty trailer came bouncing up the lane. I smoothed my hair down and tucked in my shirt.

Travis moved in behind me. I heard a scramble in the loft, and then they were all there.

I didn't want them there. I wanted to have Twila all to myself.

"Is that Twila?" Jen asked.

"Scoot over!" Maggie whispered.

Twila stopped the truck, got out, and started toward us.

"Wow!" Ray said, sounding wide awake now. He lowered his voice to a whisper. "Man, if that's what you're going to look like someday, Scoop, we've got to stay in touch!"

"Hey!" Carla elbowed Ray into silence. "She really does look just like you, Scoop," she whispered.

"That's pretty amazing," Travis said. "Look at her eyes."

When I could get my legs to move, I walked up to Twila.

"It's nice," she said, her gaze taking in the paddock, the barn, the pastures. "You're right, Scoop. I can see why a horse would consider this home."

Behind me, somebody cleared his or her throat.

Twila nodded to Maggie, like she remembered her from Dalton's. She smiled at everybody else.

I knew I should introduce them. I probably should have given her a tour of Horsefeathers. But all I wanted to do was get out of there. "I'll get Orphan," I said. I ran past Carla and Ray to get my horse.

Twila waited where she was, and nobody else moved. Tugging Orphan behind me, I led her straight to the trailer and loaded her, closing the tailgate behind her.

"Bye!" I called, with a wave to everybody as

I slid into the passenger seat of Twila's truck.

Travis waved.

"Call me later!" Maggie shouted.

Twila circled the trailer and drove away. I didn't look back. Finally, I took a deep breath. We were on our way. And I knew deep in my bones that after today, my life would never be the same.

13

I kept stealing glances at Twila on the drive to Cherokee Bend, trying to discover more evidence of motherhood. If she were my mother, she must have been really young when she had me. I remembered Emma and Ben Coop looking older than Twila, and my memories were already more than eight years old.

I felt like my brain was split down the middle, divided in two like a horse's brain. The left brain and right brain of a horse act almost independently. It may be okay with one side of the brain to let a rider mount from the left side, but mounting from the right side is out of the question. Some horses couldn't care less if a groom shaves the inside of one ear, but they put up a fight when somebody tries the same clippers on the other ear.

That's what I felt like—split down the middle. *See*, one side of my brain reasoned, *Twila Twopennies can't be your mother. She's too young.* Then the other side of my brain argued, *She's your mother all right. That's why she had to put you up for adoption—she was just too young to raise you herself.*

Twila was talking. "So you and Orphan may need to bring in the broodmares. And I'd like you to work with Lefty too."

As she talked, I couldn't take my eyes off her hands, sunned and slender, with skin like bronzed silk over bone. All her fingernails were the same length, as if she filed them instead of biting them like Dotty and I did.

Dotty's hands gripping the wheel always remind me of B.C.'s dried Playdough. Her chubby fingers never leave the ten and two o'clock position on the steering wheel, as if they were molded down. I glanced at my own hands. *They're definitely more like Twila's*, said one side of my brain. *Look at those long fingers, with so much more bone than flesh*. Then my other side kicked in: *You sure bite your nails like Dotty!*

We crossed the railroad tracks without stopping, and instinctively I grabbed the door handle and glanced both ways. Patches of fog still swirled across the road in low-lying places. "Did I scare you?" Twila asked, grinning. "Trains hardly ever run back here."

I forced a laugh. "Dotty, my aunt, stops at every single railroad track. I think she honestly expects a train every time and is surprised when it doesn't come."

We passed the stretch of dandelions growing

thick in the ditch. "Did you ever wonder why people think dandelions are weeds instead of flowers?" Twila asked. "If I owned a state, I'd make the state flower the dandelion."

There I was thinking about dandelions, and she read my mind! "Yes!" I said. "I mean, *I* think they're flowers—beautiful flowers."

I had to find a way to ask her what I needed to ask her. I figured we were about halfway to Cherokee Bend. I might not get a better chance to talk to her. "Um … do you have an aunt?" *An aunt?* I couldn't believe I'd asked that. That wasn't one of the questions Maggie and I had rehearsed!

"An aunt?" Twila looked at me puzzled. "Yes," she said slowly. "Two of them actually. Though I haven't seen them in years."

Think! I told myself. Go on. You can't sound any stupider. "Colt said you grew up around here?"

She sighed, as if thinking of it made her tired. "I went to school here. Whether or not I grew up … that's another question. I came back five, almost six, years ago and started the ranch."

I would have been 10. It was the year I got caught shoplifting, and also the year Dotty shared God's love and forgiveness with me. What if Twila had come back to look for me? What if she'd found me then? What would my life have been like?

I'd gone this far. I might as well go for broke while I could still get words past the lump in my throat. "Kids?" I asked hoarsely.

Did her face change for an instant, turn sad and longing? Or was I imagining it? She didn't answer.

"I'm sorry," I said. "I don't mean to be so nosy. Colt said he thought you were married once. It's none of my business."

"Colt, huh?" she muttered. I hoped I hadn't gotten him in trouble. But if it made her tell me, I didn't care.

"Yes, I was married once, for a little while, a long time ago." Her dark brown eyes focused on the road, and she seemed to be somewhere else in her thoughts. With my father? I wondered?

My father. What had happened to him? Was he still alive? I hadn't even allowed myself to think about him. What was he like? Was he American Indian too? Did he love horses? Maybe he had died a tragic death? Was that it? Was I going to lose another father before I'd even had the chance to know him?

Twila Twopennies shook her head as if to wake herself from a dream. "That was all such a long time ago. We got a divorce less than a year after we were married."

Then he was probably still alive! Of course they'd divorced. They probably couldn't get over their mistake of giving me up for adoption.

Suddenly I wanted to cry for them—as if *they* were the children and *I'd* left them.

The pieces were fitting together. The *Yes! You're Twila's daughter* side of my brain was winning. We were almost to her ranch. I turned to Twila, took a deep breath, and prayed. *This is it, Lord. Help me get the words out. I have to know the truth about my family.*

"Twila," I began, "I have to ask you something, something important. I think you might be my—"

"What the h—?" She slammed on her brakes.

I heard Orphan stomp in the trailer. Then through the fog, Colt appeared in the middle of the lane. He was waving his arms. He ran up to Twila, and she rolled down her window.

"What's the matter?" she asked.

"It's Queenie, the Knowlton's broodmare," Colt said. His sleeves were rolled up, and he was sweaty and out of breath. "She lost her foal."

"No!" Twila's slender hand knotted into a fist as she hit the steering wheel. "What happened, Colt? Was it stillborn? She had a week to go! I should have brought her in from the pasture." She banged the dashboard and cursed under her breath.

"I'm not sure what happened," Colt said. He looked a little afraid of her. "There's no sign of the foal. The mare must have dropped it last night in the out pasture."

"Get in," Twila told him gruffly.

I was glad I wasn't in Colt's shoes. I wasn't used to being around swearing. Colt ran around to my side, and I scooted closer to Twila as she put the truck in gear. I might as well have been invisible, which for the moment was just fine with me. I stared at my hands while Colt talked across me to Twila.

"The mare came running in with the herd right after you drove off. As soon as I saw her, I knew she'd had her foal. Sam and I ran right out to the pasture and searched everywhere for it, but we couldn't find a trace."

"D— coyotes!" Twila swore again. "I'd like to shoot every wild animal in the state!"

"But—but are you sure?" I asked weakly.

Colt looked down at me like he'd just noticed I was sitting there. "I think I know when a broodmare's dropped her foal. In laymen's terms—make that laywoman's terms—she was fat. Now she's skinny."

"I don't mean that," I said, not looking up at him. I turned to Twila. She stopped the trailer close to the barn. "Couldn't we look again? My grandad used to say coyotes hardly ever went after the foals. People just stopped looking too soon and blamed foxes or coyotes. Maybe the foal is still out there?"

"We looked!" Colt sounded like he thought I was accusing him.

"I know. It's just, with the fog and all. ..." I turned to plead with Twila. I couldn't stand the thought of a defenseless foal out there alone in the fog, motherless. "Isn't it worth another look? Please?"

Twila had turned off the engine, but she still held the wheel stiff-armed. "Okay. Let's spread out and have another look."

Colt sighed, but he didn't try to talk her out of it. I had a feeling that nobody talked Twila Twopennies out of anything.

Twila checked the mare while Colt and I waited in the mist of the paddock. The mare was a beautiful, gray Arabian, and she had definitely foaled. Her belly was flat, and she was dripping milk from her teats, where her foal should have been nursing.

"We were going to keep her in the small pasture closest to the barn," Colt explained. "But she put up such a fit when we tried to separate her from those two geldings and that mare over there, we decided to wait until today to bring her in."

Twila joined us. "She's fine, but she hasn't nursed. Even if the foal had been born alive, I don't see how—"

"Then we better hurry," I said. I ran back and unloaded Orphan. "I can see better if I'm up on Orphan," I said, holding the lead rope and swinging myself up on her bare back.

Colt whispered something to Twila, but she

shook her head. "This way, Scoop," she called. "Colt and I will walk straight to the far fence on foot. You can ride around the perimeter."

A mist hung over the pasture as we hunted up and down the acreage. I prayed God would help us find the foal, and it would be okay and get back safely to its mother. I wondered if Twila and Colt prayed too.

I couldn't believe Colt had appeared right when I was going to ask Twila straight out if I could be her daughter. Part of me wanted to gallop up to her right then and there and demand an answer. But the other part of me knew we had to find the foal now before it was too late.

We walked the pasture top to bottom, side to side. After over an hour, Colt hollered, "I told you! We've been all over this pasture."

I turned Orphan around, and something in the grass caught my eye. Filtered sunlight lit up a shiny spot near a fallen log at the base of a hill. I rode over to inspect it. At first, I thought it might be a piece of plastic. Then I saw what it was. "Twila!" I yelled. "Come here! I've found the placenta."

Twila and Colt jogged over and stared down at the slimy remains of the afterbirth. A foal had definitely been born right at this spot.

"That's the end of that then," Twila said. "My only hope was that Queenie managed to have her foal somewhere else and jump back into the pasture. But she obviously had it here. Some d— varmint must have dragged it off. Come on. We've wasted enough time." She started back toward the barn with Colt beside her.

"We can't leave!" I cried. "She could still be out here. You can't walk off and leave her—not until we know for sure!" I was trying hard not to cry, but my voice shook.

"I'm late for my next lesson," Colt said to Twila, ignoring me.

"Let it go, Scoop," Twila said. "These things happen. We've got work to do."

"Please!" I couldn't accept it. Orphan must have sensed how upset I was. She nickered so low only I could have heard her.

"Scoop," Twila started, "I have a ranch to run and—" She broke off and sighed. "Oh all right. Ten minutes. Then I need you in the paddock. Understand?"

"Thank you," I said. "I leaned on Orphan's neck and whispered, "Find that foal, Orphan. Fast!"

14

Orphan cantered, and I strained to see through the mist. *Please, God*, I prayed. *Help us find the foal. Don't let it be dead. Help me bring it to its mother.*

For the first few minutes I retraced my steps, moving up and down through the grass, focusing near the placenta. At that end of the pasture a hill ran right up to a wire fence. All of us had searched the area. I rode Orphan up the hill to get a better view. At the top, we stood still. Orphan craned her head around. Her nostrils widened. Then she let out a high-pitched neigh, followed by a little squeal.

I couldn't see or hear any signs of the foal, so I tried to urge Orphan back down the hill. But Orphan stood her ground.

"Come on, Girl," I pleaded. "We've only got a minute left."

She whinnied again, and then I heard a tiny answering whinny, so faint it might have been the wind or a cat or a million other things. The sound came from behind us.

I slid off Orphan and eased my way down the hill, slipping, then catching myself. Orphan took off down the front of the hill and circled round, getting to the wire fence before me. It didn't seem possible that there was room enough between fence and hill for a mouse, much less a foal.

The mist cleared for just an instant, and I spotted something in the weeds—a dark gray, furry, wet mass. It was the foal, and it was alive! I wanted to yell for help, but I couldn't risk frightening the baby.

"We've got you now, little one," I murmured as I leaned down and stroked the foal's neck, feeling his warmth in my fingertips. It was a boy, a colt, and his heart was beating as fast as mine. "Why were you hiding in the mist, you little Misty?"

The colt craned his head around to look at me. Mucus covered his nostrils and mouth, and much of the membrane still wrapped the poor abandoned foal in a cocoon, making him look like he was shrinkwrapped in plastic.

"You poor baby," I said. "Did you roll down the hill? Are you hurt?" Why had his mother left him out here like that? The foal needed her to lick off the membrane as part of the bonding process. But it was too late now. I'd have to wipe him clean.

Orphan stuck her head through the tiny space and began licking the foal's haunches. I pulled off my boots, removed my socks, and put my boots back on. As Orphan licked little Misty, I wiped the colt with my socks, muttering nonsense to him all the while. He was lying on his side, but he jerked his head up. I kept rubbing his face gently until I felt him relax. Then I continued rubbing until he rested his head on my knees.

I needed to get Misty to his mother as soon as possible. Colt and Twila would come looking for me pretty soon. "Help!" I yelled.

The colt jerked. I didn't want to scare him. I know that what happens to a colt during the hour or hours before he gets to his feet can make a lifetime of difference.

I rubbed his ears and mouth and nose and felt him calm down again. I stroked his back and legs, lifted his hooves and tapped each one. Twila and Colt still hadn't come back.

"We can't wait any longer," I told Orphan. "We have to get this guy to his mother."

Orphan nickered to Misty as I got to my feet and reached for the foal. He was wedged against the fence. No wonder he hadn't been able to get up by himself. I almost had hold of him when my boot slipped. I stumbled, and we both fell back down.

"Sorry, Misty," I murmured, getting back up. This time I braced my feet apart, kept my knees slightly bent, and lifted the foal with every ounce of strength I had. Somewhere from the back of my brain came the words from God that I remembered from Sunday school, "He shall give you strength." I thanked Him for it.

Orphan kept her nose right up to Misty's as I struggled across the pasture toward the barn. Twice I had to stop and sit down, balancing the foal across my lap. Where were Twila and Colt?

A few feet from the gate I heard a little girl holler, "Colt! Colt! Look at the girl out there!"

When Colt spotted me, he opened the gate and came running. I gladly handed over the foal and brushed off my shirt and arms. "Where was she?" he asked.

"*He*," I corrected. "We found him on the other side of the hill, against the fence. Poor thing. Why would Queenie leave him out there like that?"

"It's her first foal," he said, carrying Misty through to the paddock. He ordered two young girls back to their horses. "Queenie doesn't know how to mother. She was probably relieved to have the foal disappear. She'd rather run with her herd."

"That's terrible!" I said. "And we better change her mind fast. Misty needs his mother's milk."

Twila came running over, a huge grin spreading across her face. "And who do we have here?" she asked, checking the colt's pulse, then peering into his eyes and mouth.

"This is Misty," Colt said. He laughed when the colt squirmed at the sound of his name. "Hey, Misty," Colt said. "Don't forget this. I can carry you around any time I please, even when you're all grown up." He winked over at me, and I grinned back.

Colt set the colt down in the paddock. Misty stood tent-like, his long legs spread out. Orphan walked up to him and continued licking. Then the colt took a wobbly step, then another. I glanced up at Orphan, who had never looked so proud. She nodded her head, an approving *yes*.

"He's a beauty!" Twila exclaimed. "He looks like the sire, doesn't he, Colt? The Knowltons are going to be happy with this one."

"What should we do with him?" Colt asked.

"He needs his first feeding, the colostrum. Let's get the mare." Twila jogged off toward the small pasture, and Colt followed her. I could see Queenie, the mare, in the middle of her buddies, grazing as if nothing at all had happened to her today.

Misty was adorable. He sniffed a dandelion, fell into a sit-up position, pushed himself back up and sniffed again. His mother would *have* to love him!

Twila and Colt approached the mare from opposite sides, threading among the rest of the herd. Colt reached Queenie first and locked his arms around her neck. "Got her!" he called.

Twila ran up with a halter and slipped it on. She and Colt worked like a team, but the mare's eyes shone white with fright or anger. I wanted to help, but I couldn't leave Misty. I knelt beside the colt and held him firm while Colt and Twila walked Queenie toward us.

Orphan stood her ground and watched with Misty as Queenie was led closer and closer. About six feet away, Queenie put on her brakes.

"Come on now," Colt said, pulling on the lead rope.

Queenie jerked back from him. Then she reared, pawing the air. Twila and Colt stepped aside, but Colt held on to the rope.

"Easy, Girl," Twila said in a soothing tone.

Queenie reared again. She flattened her ears and snorted.

"What's the matter with her?" I asked, feeling Misty's pain. What would the poor colt think now?

"You've never been a mother before, have you, Queenie?" Twila said, talking to her horse instead of to me. She stroked Queenie's neck until the rearing eased off, getting smaller and shorter, and finally stopping. "This is your baby," Twila said, scratching the mare's jaw. "I know, Queenie. That little one is going to be a heap of trouble, but that can't be helped. Give him a drink now, okay?"

It seemed to be working. Twila took the lead

rope from Colt, and he stepped back. "That's my Girl," Twila said. Softly, to me, she said, "Scoop, you step back so Misty can find the milk."

I took several steps backwards and had to pull on Orphan's halter to get her to move away from the foal.

"A little farther," Twila coaxed, as she led Queenie nearer to her foal. "There's a good mom now."

But Queenie changed her mind again and stopped in her tracks. Her forelegs stiffened. Twila faced the mare and pulled on the rope. She turned her back and tried to tug the mare after her. But it was no use.

"Colt," she called, "give me a hand."

Colt grabbed Queenie's halter. By sheer brute strength and determination, the two of them got her to step forward.

"There you go," Twila said, grunting like the mare.

Suddenly Queenie squealed, as if she only just now understood what was happening to her. Instead of pulling back this time, she bolted forward. With her ears back and teeth bared, there was nothing motherly about the mare. Twila leaped aside, as Queenie charged straight at Misty.

15

"Heyah! Get!" Colt ran at Queenie, screaming and hollering.

The horse pivoted and tore to the far end of the paddock, bucking and twisting like a bronco.

Orphan and I closed around Misty. His eyes were wide, and he trembled all over. The foal let Orphan nuzzle him and breathe into his nostrils.

Twila walked up. "That d— mare!" she cursed. "I could twitch her and get her back, but I don't think she'd hold still to nurse."

"I can't believe she'd do that!" I said, running my finger lightly over the foal's back.

Colt came over to us. "Now what do we do, Twila?" He frowned at Queenie, who was talking with a sorrel gelding over the paddock fence.

"I think if I hold her, she'll let you take her milk," Twila told him. "That's the most important thing right now. The colt needs that colostrum."

I knew how important it was for Misty to get the colostrum, or first milk. If he didn't get it, he wouldn't get the immunities to fight off diseases.

Besides, I didn't know how long he had lain out in the pasture. He needed the protein and fat and sugar to live and to stay warm. Twila was right. We'd have to get Misty fed however we could. But I wouldn't rest until he was able to nurse from his own mother.

"*If* that mare will let me get her milk," Colt began, "should we force-feed the colt with the stomach tube?"

"No!" I shouted, so loud they both turned to me. "I'm sorry. I mean, I'll feed Misty with a bottle if you can get Queenie's milk. He shouldn't have to have a tube stuck in him!"

Twila cocked her head to one side and narrowed her eyes at me. "Do you know what you're letting yourself in for, Scoop?" she asked. "One bottle won't do it."

"I know," I said. "I bottle-fed Orphan when she was a foal." But my horse's mother had been dead. That's why Orphan had needed a bottle. "I'll be responsible for feeding Misty until his mother comes around. I promise."

"In small bottle doses, that colt won't drink more than a few ounces at a time." Twila seemed to be sizing up Misty, as well as me. "And he's going to need about 10 percent of his body weight in mare's milk. Queenie may not come around, you know. That means this foal is going to need about seven or eight pounds of milk every day for at least three days before we switch him to Foal Lac. You'll have to feed him every hour through the night."

"I'll do it," I said. "I will, Twila." I wouldn't mind doing it. I wanted to feed Misty. But Twila was wrong. Queenie *would* come around. There was no way I was going to let that mare reject her own baby.

Misty sidled up to Orphan, and Orphan put her head over the colt's neck, protecting him. I waited, prayed, hoped Twila would understand.

Finally she said, "Colt, I guess you better get some milk from that mare. Scoop, you'll have to sleep over tonight. Is that all right?"

"No problem," I said, wondering how much of a problem it was actually going to be. I knew how Dotty felt about Sundays. But that was just too bad. I was doing this no matter what.

"I'll get a bottle," Twila said, turning to go. "Colt, you get to work on Queenie."

Queenie surprised all of us by not putting up a fuss when Colt squeezed out her milk. She didn't mind being milked by humans, but she wouldn't let her own foal nurse. Colt got enough milk to fill several small bottles and a larger container Twila brought out.

As he handed me the bottle and I knelt in front of Misty, my mind flashed back to the day I'd offered Orphan a bottle. Orphan had probably been just about Misty's size, although to me, a 3-year-old kid, she had seemed huge. But I wasn't afraid of Orphan, ever. It was the day Emma and Benjamin Coop brought me home from the adoption agency. I can still picture Orphan lying on her side, refusing to drink from the bottle Grandad pushed at her. I'd walked right over, grabbed the bottle, and fed her. Two orphans finding each other.

And now Orphan, fully grown, stood over me as I held the bottle out to this little colt, who was no better off than an orphan. Misty's mother had rejected him for now, but I was determined to do everything in my power to get mother and foal back together again.

Twila watched us. I thought of something Travis had said about adoption and forgiveness. Somewhere along the line, I knew I'd forgiven my mother. If Twila was really my mother, I knew she must have had a good reason for giving me up. I wanted Twila right now to be thinking the same thoughts I was thinking—about mothers and forgiveness in Christ.

Misty licked the bottle. Then he took the nipple in his lips and began to suck on it, drinking, his neck stretched out, taking in the nourishment that would get him through this. I smiled up at Twila. Her eyes looked misted over—I was sure of it. She turned and walked quickly toward the house.

"What's with her?" Colt asked, staring.

I shrugged. Could Twila be remembering

the birth I couldn't remember?

"Colt! There you are!" a low female voice rang out.

At the fence, half a dozen girls waved to Colt as if he were a movie star. I did a double take at the tallest girl. I recognized that deep, trying-to-sound-sexy voice. She wore an expensive English riding habit. Her long, bleached-blonde hair hung in bouncy curls from under her black riding helmet.

"Ursula?" I said. What was Stephen Dalton's girlfriend doing taking riding lessons from Colt? Ursula always looks down her long, slender nose at Horsefeathers and at Orphan and at me. But I'll grant her one thing—she's a strong rider. No way was she here for the lessons.

Ursula's wave hung limp in the air as it dawned on her who I was. Her thick, pouty lips made a perfect little *o*.

I waved back as if Ursula and I were best friends. "Hey, Ursula!" I shouted. "Imagine meeting you here!"

She lifted her fingers slightly in the weakest wave I'd ever gotten. I'd let her wonder whether I'd tell her boyfriend on her. I wouldn't—but she didn't know that.

"Guess duty calls," Colt said. "Will you be okay here?"

I nodded, conscious that every girl watching us would have given anything to be me right then.

"When you're done, you could move over there." Colt pointed to a shady spot in the paddock, against the stable and next to the lesson arena. "I'll bring you another bottle every hour."

Misty didn't quite finish the little bottle of colostrum. I wasn't worried. I knew how tiny a foal's stomach is. He needed a lot of milk, but he couldn't handle very much at a time. That's why I'd have to spend the night.

Spend the night! Dotty! I was going to have to phone her sooner or later.

I waited until Colt brought out the next bottle. While Misty slurped and sucked the nipple, and Orphan nodded approvingly, I rehearsed what I'd say to Dotty.

Leaving Misty under the watchful eye of Orphan, I ran to the house to use the phone. Twila was coming out as I trotted up the stone walkway. She gave me permission to use the phone and headed for the barn to get a stall ready for Misty and me.

I stepped into the empty house and had to stop in the doorway. It smelled like home—not Dotty's home. Dotty makes coffee with hot water and spoonfuls of instant coffee. What I was smelling was the real thing—brewed coffee, and something like fresh baked bread. I'm not sure if I'd ever really smelled it before, but it was a familiar smell just the same.

I dialed Dotty's. I counted the rings—six,

seven, eight. Then I remembered. It was Saturday and Dotty would still be at the Hy-Klas. Just as well, I thought, as the phone kept ringing. B.C. could give Dotty my message, and I wouldn't have to argue over the phone.

I gave my brother enough time to climb down off of the roof and still get to the phone. I was about to hang up when the phone stopped ringing and a tiny voice said, "Hello."

"B.C.!" I said. "What took you so long? Were you on the roof?"

"No." He sounded a million miles away. The life had gone out of his voice, like it did when he was in the depression part of his manic depression.

I couldn't help B.C. Not now. Not this time. "B.C., is Dotty home yet?"

"No."

I should have asked him what was wrong, but I had to get back to the paddock. Maybe I'd have a chance to talk to Twila while she was in the stables. "B.C.," I said, "this is important. Can you give Dotty a message for me?"

He didn't answer, but I could hear him breathing. He was still there.

"Okay," I went on. "Tell Dotty I have to spend the night at Twila's and—"

"No!" B.C. screamed so loud into the phone it hurt my ear. "I want you home!"

"Listen, B.C." I tried to keep calm. He

could hang up on me at any minute. "There's a newborn colt here who needs me to—"

"*I* need you!" B.C. screamed. "I need you to come home! Why do you like it there so much? You should be here!"

"B.C.," I pleaded. "You have to listen. If I don't stay here and feed this little colt all during the night, he'll die." Maybe I was stretching the truth a little. Colt or anybody else could have fed Misty. But I had to make my point.

"I don't like you there!" B.C. cried. "I want you here. I have math homework, and Tommy Zucker said Grace said I'm weird and—"

"Could we do this later, B.C.?" I begged. "Listen, I have to stay here tonight ... and tomorrow too." Might as well get it all out at once. "Tell Dotty I'll be at Cherokee Bend. Got it? Write it down, B.C."

"You have to go to church!" B.C. yelled. It was exactly what Dotty would say.

"Tell Dotty I'll read my Bible out here and pray and everything. I'll call tomorrow." I hung up before B.C. could think of another argument. The click of the phone brought instant relief, like turning off a rotten show on TV.

As I jogged back to the stable, I tried to put Dotty and B.C. and everything else at the other end of the phone out of my mind. It was amazingly easy.

16

I ran straight to the paddock and snapped a rope on Queenie's halter. It was worth another try to get mother and foal together, even though I knew it was probably too soon to try it again. I looked around for Twila and felt an almost physical disappointment in my chest when I didn't see her.

Colt was teaching a small class of girls about my age to jump over low hurdles in the arena. I watched them as I led Queenie to the corner of the fence, the closest spot to her foal, who lay in the grass next to Orphan. Mother and foal were only a few feet apart now, separated by a low, wooden fence. I let Queenie stand and gaze at Misty, but she didn't seem the least bit interested. When I tried to pull her head over the fence so she'd be even closer, she jerked away.

"Nice one, Amanda!" Colt called in a warm voice he'd never used on me. "If I were the judge, you'd have a big trophy right now."

I studied Colt. He was nice enough to me, but it was clear he thought of me as just one of the guys, one of the hands.

"They're all in love with him." I hadn't heard Twila behind me. The sound of her voice startled me. She unhooked Queenie, and the mare trotted off, grateful for the freedom.

I looked back at the arena and saw Colt helping the prettiest of the equestrians dismount. He kept his hands around her waist much longer than he had to. They were laughing, their noses an inch apart.

"Colt flirts a lot," Twila said quietly. "But he doesn't mean much by it."

"He doesn't flirt with me," I said. As soon as I said the words, I wanted them back. I turned to face Twila and tried to pull off a light laugh. It didn't work. "N-not that I want him to flirt with me or anything."

"Well," Twila said, "if you ever change your mind, if you want any hints in the flirting department, you know where to come."

I couldn't look at her. I wasn't sure why—maybe it was the idea of flirting with Colt, or maybe the idea of asking for flirting lessons from someone who might well be my mother. "I better get back to Colt—I mean, to *the* colt, to Misty," I stammered.

Misty and Orphan were standing right where I'd left them, in the shade behind the main barn. Orphan whinnied to me as I walked up to them. Then Misty nickered too, and came trotting, then half-cantering toward me. He seemed to have grown in the minutes I'd been away from him.

I decided this was a good time as any to get him used to being handled. Jen Zucker calls the way I handled Lefty "imprinting." She'd read all about how modern horse trainers like to get foals used to things they'll face when they're older. Jen, Maggie, Carla, and I had talked about raising foals. But mostly, I just do what comes natural to me, and then Jen has a name for it.

I found a comfortable spot in the soft grass where I could lean against a maple tree and still see Colt giving lessons at one end of the arena. "Come here, Misty!" I called.

One ear pointed straight at me, and the other twitched up, to the side, then up again.

"Bring him over here, Orphan," I commanded.

Orphan stepped slowly toward me, and the foal followed. When they got close enough, I reached up to pet Misty. I scratched his back until he swayed with my hand movements. When he'd almost dozed off, I gently pulled him onto my lap. He squirmed at first, but I held him firm. In a second he calmed, as comfy as Dogless cat curled in my lap.

I repeated everything I'd done in the pasture, starting with his head and moving down to his haunches and legs. This time he didn't resist at all.

Turning him over onto his side was a little tougher. But once settled, he closed his eyes while I repeated the whole process. "Now, Misty," I said as I ran my finger around his ear, "this will make you used to having your ears shaved one day—if humans do that to you."

I stuck my finger in his mouth and felt him suck as I stroked his tongue and felt inside his mouth. "And you'll remember this when it's time to bridle you." Bending each leg, then straightening them one at a time, over and over, I murmured, "Your farrier is going to love me. Doc Vicki, a veterinarian I know, says the locals can always tell when I've handled a horse as a colt. They're the easiest horses to shoe." Again, I tapped each hoof on the bottom.

I rubbed his withers and back, upper shoulder, and rib cage. "One day we'll saddle you, and you won't even care," I said. "You'll be so used to the touch of something on your back, your horse trainer will think somebody's already ridden you."

I was just about to go look for Misty's next bottle, when I glanced up. My heart stopped as I looked from face to face to face—all staring down at me from the arena fence, from the barn, from the drive. Parents, student riders, dozens of people had been watching me, listening to me baby-talk Misty. I had been the center ring of a three-ring circus, and I hadn't even known it! I wanted to crawl in a hole and hide.

I heard one loud single clap. Then another clap. I turned and saw Colt and Twila in the middle of the spectators. They were applauding. Then everybody broke into applause. I glanced over my shoulder and out in the paddock to make sure they weren't clapping for somebody else.

Colt and Twila climbed the fence and walked toward me. "That was wonderful!" Twila said. "I've read about imprinting foals, but I've never seen it. Where did you learn how?"

"I didn't," I said, not at all sure how to handle this attention. I didn't care about anybody's applause, except Twila's—and maybe Colt's.

"I want you to teach me how to do what you just did with that colt, Scoop," Colt said. He scratched his head, showing sweat half-moons under his armpits. On him, even that looked good.

"Colt! What about us?" I recognized Ursula's not-so-low-and-sexy whine.

He handed me another bottle and ran back to the fence to finish his lessons. "Later, Scoop!" he called back.

"Scoop," Twila said. She looked proud of me. Her face was so serious that for a second I believed she was going to tell me the truth, that I was her daughter.

"Yes?" My voice cracked.

"I want to ask you something, but I don't

know how you'll feel about it," she said.

My hands were trembling, and Misty didn't like it. He squirmed off my lap and trotted to Orphan. "Go on," I said, not daring to look at Twila, afraid she'd vanish if I did.

"Do you think ... would you like to spend more time out here at Cherokee Bend? I have a job for you."

And just like that, the moment was gone. Something cold as a winter's breeze blew through me, taking away the instant of hope and revelation. I felt like a barrel-racing quarter horse forced to change leads. I'd gone from Twila's daughter to her hired hand in the flick of a horse's tail.

I managed to nod.

"Good!" she said. "I want you to work with Queenie's foal—more than just feeding him. And I want you to work with Queenie. I need that mare to accept her foal. I don't know if she'll feel like nursing Misty or not. But even if she won't nurse, I need her to *act* like a mother—and I'd like to see it happen before next Saturday. Knowltons want that mare to be a broodmare. They plan on getting lots of foals out of her. When they come to see the foal next week, they're going to want to see a happy couple—mare and foal. And I think you're just the girl to pull it off. What do you say, Scoop? Will you give it your best try?"

"Sure," I said, trying not to let the disappointment sink in. But it felt as if Twila and I had been standing on the edge of a cliff that would take us to a whole new world. And now she'd backed away again, putting more distance between us with every word she spoke.

"Great!" She walked back to the house, and I felt like I was being left all over again.

The rest of the afternoon, I hung out with Orphan and Misty. Colt helped me catch Queenie and try three more times to introduce her to Misty. But each attempt at nursing was worse than the one before. The mare would let us lead her as close as a couple of horse lengths away, but no closer. I wasn't about to give in though. I started to feel that if I could succeed at getting Queenie and Misty together, somehow Twila and I could find each other too.

Misty drank milk every hour. He let me put a tiny halter on him. I left it on for a few minutes, took it off, put it on, took it off. Between bottle feedings, I watched Colt give lessons and Twila talk to parents. Several of the girls' fathers seemed to have as big of crushes on Twila as their daughters did on Colt. I liked it when students waved at me like I was part of the ranch, like this was my home.

"So how does it feel to be famous?" Colt asked, coming over to the fence after the last students left.

"*You're* asking me?" I said.

"Hey, you were the topic of conversation around here all day." He bumped his shoulder into mine.

I looked away and spotted Twila standing beside one of the cars. She'd changed into a long, brown-and-gold dress that made her skin look darker and her hair even more beautiful. She was talking to a man who could have starred in a Western, he was so handsome.

"That's Hank," Colt offered.

Watching the way she put her hand on his arm and leaned her ear in close to him, I felt something I couldn't put my finger on. Then I realized—I was jealous. Jealous for my father. "Is ... is he her boyfriend?"

Colt laughed. "Good question. He'd probably say yes. I don't think she would though. Twila would probably say he's Wednesday night."

I looked up at him. His tanned face wrinkled at the mouth, bringing out his dimple. "Wednesday night?" I asked.

"Twila lets Hank take her Western line dancing on Wednesdays," Colt explained. "Let's see. Friday night is Brent, usually fancy dinner out—sometimes a movie. Sunday could be Bill or this other guy from Kennsington."

"So she doesn't ... she isn't ... you know," I said, stumbling over my tongue. "She isn't like planning to marry any of them?"

"Twila?" Colt glanced over at her. Twila was waving good-bye to Hank and his daughter. "Not likely. I don't think she'll ever get married."

Again, I wanted to say. Maybe she wouldn't get married again because she still loved my father.

"What about Saturday?" I asked. "Where's she going tonight?"

"Man!" Colt said, glancing at his watch. "I forgot. I was supposed to tell you she wanted us to have dinner with her at the house. Sorry. You're staying the night anyway, right?"

"Yeah." This was too wonderful! Dinner with Colt and my mother. The cautious side of my brain was barely whispering now, feebly muttering, *Don't forget. You don't know she's your mother*. I was changing leads again, this time from hired hand back to daughter. True, Colt was just a hired hand, and he was invited. But I took my invitation as the first step in becoming family. What better way to get our feet wet than to share a meal? Maybe over dinner, with nobody there but Colt and me, she'd open up and talk about the child she put up for adoption.

"It will just be you and Twila and my dad and me," Colt said. I must have looked shocked because he added, "My parents have been divorced for years. Mom lives in Nevada. Dad has the honor of being Twila's Tuesday Man normally. But Twila invited all of us, and Dad wouldn't miss dinner with Twila."

Colt's dad would be there. I didn't like it, but it didn't mean I had to change leads again. So he would be there. Colt said Twila and his dad had gone to high school together. Maybe Mr. Cleveland had met my dad. Things were changing so fast I had to gallop just to keep up.

Twila waved us in. "Scoop, you can clean up for dinner in here!"

I headed for the house.

A long screech cut the twilight's calm. It came again: *Scree-ee—ch*! Twila covered her ears and frowned across the yard in the direction of the horrible noise.

No! It can't be! I knew that sound. I'd heard it a thousand times.

I made myself look. Dotty's battered blue Chevy bounced and skidded around the corner and up the drive, the brakes squealing like scared mice.

Behind me Colt said, "What on earth?"

I wanted to run into the house, to pretend I had no idea what this was, who this was. This couldn't be happening! Dotty. What if she'd driven here to get me? She'd ruin everything!

17

Gravel crunched and brakes squealed as Dotty ground to a halt in front of Twila Twopennies. She beeped the horn twice.

We heard you, Dotty, I thought. It was too embarrassing! What was I going to do now?

Whatever I want! I determined. Dotty couldn't make me go with her. I was staying at Cherokee Bend no matter what she said.

"It's okay, Twila," I said, trotting over to Dotty's car. "It's just my aunt. I'll handle it." *Please go back inside the house.*

Dotty didn't wait for me to reach her open window. She opened the door, plopped one foot out, then the other, and finally pushed herself to her feet. "My, my, ain't this the cat's pajamas!" she exclaimed.

"The cat's pajamas?" I heard Colt repeat.

I ran up to Dotty. "What are you doing here?" I waved to Twila as if everything were just fine. "Dotty, I'm staying all night here. Didn't B.C. tell you? I have to! The colt will die if I don't feed it all night."

"B.C. done told me, Scoop, more or less. You know how I feel about Sundays and church and all—"

"Dotty, I'm staying!" I shot the words out between my teeth, so Twila couldn't see how angry I was. "You're not my mother, and you can't make me leave!"

Dotty's nose twitched, and her eyes blinked. It was a second before she answered. "I-I was going to say that I reckon the Lord will understand just this once—seein's how that there colt is countin' on you."

Yes!

"Hey there!" Dotty said to my right shoulder.

I turned and was horrified to see Twila standing behind me.

"This must be Aunt Dotty?" Twila asked, when I didn't introduce them.

"Um ... Twila," I said, "this is Dotty Eberhart. Dotty, Twila Twopennies."

"It's real nice of you to have Scoop sleep over," Dotty said.

"Actually," Twila said, a little stiffly, "she's the one doing us the favor. I'm paying her," she added quickly.

"Oh!" Dotty turned her back on us to reach for something in her car. Her black pants had a split in the seam. Her orange Hy-Klas apron had hidden the tear when she was standing up, but now her white underpants puffed through the black slit like frosting from an Oreo cookie.

"Let me help," I said, moving in to hide her backside.

"I got it," she said, grunting with the effort, then wiggling herself back out of the car. She held out a plastic Hy-Klas grocery bag to me. "Thought you might need clean underwear and a change of clothes. I stuck in your toothbrush."

Embarrassed, I took the bag quickly.

"You ain't got your Bible!" she exclaimed, slapping her forehead with her palm. "Twila, you got an extry Bible Scoop can borrow?"

"It's okay, Dotty," I whispered.

"I-I don't know," Twila said. "There might be one somewhere around here. In the attic maybe?"

Dotty's face looked like a horse had stepped on her foot, as if it hurt her that Twila didn't know exactly where her Bible was. "Hey!" She wheeled around and repeated her burrowing routine into the depths of her car. When she backed out, she had her old, battered Bible in one hand. "You can borrow mine. I got me another at home. I plumb forgot I had this here one with me. Thank You for reminding me!"

I knew that last thank-you had been directed to God, but Twila wouldn't know.

I put my arm around Dotty's shoulder and guided her back toward the driver's seat. "Thanks for bringing the—the stuff, Dotty," I said. "I'll call you tomorrow."

She craned her head around to take in the ranch. "The good Lord sure done you generous with this here ranch, didn't He!" Dotty declared.

"I—I guess so," Twila said, shifting her weight and looking at the dirt instead of at Dotty. She glanced back at Colt and exchanged grins. "Will you excuse me? I need to go back in." Twila sidestepped toward the house.

Dotty seemed to be watching Twila walk up the stone pathway. "I reckon I'd best be gettin' back to B.C.," Dotty said, tugging one pant leg, as if her only wardrobe problem was the fact that one pant leg had slid halfway to her knee and exposed the fake nylons that only reached above her ankle. "I can see you all are right in the middle of somethin', and I done got in its way."

She had one foot in her car. "I almost forgot!" she said, stepping back out. "Maggie called, and B.C. told her you was staying here and Maggie says not to worry about chores. She'd get everybody to help out tonight and tomorrow at Horsefeathers. Oh, and she said you kids is leading the Mother's Day parade. Ain't that special!"

"We'll see." I didn't think this was the best time to tell Dotty I wouldn't be in the parade. I was glad to see Colt had disappeared, probably to the house to get ready for dinner—which was all I wanted to do too.

"We're coming right along on our church float," Dotty rattled on. "B.C. is making us a big banner with that verse in Joshua: *As for me and my house, we will serve the Lord.* You remember that one. He wants to do it all by hisself. I told him to ask that little girl he's always going on about, to ask her to come over and help." She sighed and shook her head. One strand of her short, straight hair fell over her glasses. She left it there. "Poor little B.C. says that girl hates him. Nobody could hate B.C.

"And here I go again, yapping on and on when you got friends waitin' on you." Dotty finally got in and started the car. "We miss you, Scoop," she said, backing out, her brakes squeaking all the way. I'd only been gone half a day. She shouldn't have looked so sad. "Lord, take care of our little girl and her little colt," she prayed, eyes open, steering wheel turning. "You take care now."

I ran inside. Twila was cooking something that smelled wonderful, but not like anything I'd ever smelled. She stirred things around in a big skillet, using a flat, wooden spatula.

"Good," she said when I came into the kitchen. "Colt is showering in the basement. Calvin Sr. will be here in about a half hour."

"Calvin Senior?" I asked.

"Mmm hmm. Colt's father." She turned from the skillet, and her gaze swept me from head to toe. She obviously didn't like what she saw.

I looked down at my dirty feet. I'd taken my boots off outside. After wearing them sockless all day, my feet looked like I'd been wading in mud puddles. And I had no idea where I'd put my socks after using them to wipe off Misty.

"I-I'll clean up," I said, almost afraid she'd un-invite me to dinner. I rifled through the plastic bag to see what clothes Dotty had brought. The only shirt in the bag was a bright yellow T-shirt Dotty had picked up at Goodwill a year ago. I pulled it out of the bag. A huge, green, goofy-looking smiley face stared up at us as I held up the shirt. "I think I'd rather be dirty," I muttered.

"How would you like to borrow something to wear for tonight?" she asked. "I'm almost sure I can come up with something that doesn't have a smiley face, Sarah."

Most of time I hate it when anybody calls me by my real name. But when Twila said it, it sounded right. I wondered if that was what she'd named me at birth—*if* she gave me birth. I had to keep reminding myself that I really didn't know. I couldn't be sure. And even if she really was my mom, I was almost certain *she* didn't know it. Maybe going by "Scoop" had thrown her off track when she'd come looking for me.

Twila led me through a blue carpeted bedroom that was bigger than our living room. She pointed to the bathroom that was bigger than Dotty's bedroom. "Help yourself to whatever you need," Twila said. "Shampoo is in the shower. Make yourself at home."

Make yourself at home. I loved the sound of the words. Steam poured up in the shower, and I could have stayed there forever, inhaling the scent of strawberry shampoo.

When I came out of the shower, wrapped in a towel, a beautiful dress was laid out on the bed. It was long, of the same soft material as the one Twila had on, only red and brown instead of gold and brown. Twila wanted me to wear her dress.

I sat at her dressing table and smelled the bone-handled brushes. Everything smelled like violets. I took extra time brushing and braiding my hair, smoothing it back so it looked more like Twila's. When I finished, I slipped into the dress. It was too long, but one glance in the mirror surprised me at how good I looked, how much like her. When I strapped on the sandals she'd left, they fit exactly.

I crossed the room to the tall wooden dresser in the corner. The top was covered with picture frames, most filled with photos of horses. One picture looked like a glamour shot of Twila. She could have been on the cover of *Vogue* magazine. She looked beautiful. Behind it, a cardboard frame folded out, revealing a mini-photo album with dozens of photographs. I thumbed through the pictures of a little black-haired girl on a Shetland pony, on an Appaloosa, with a big Irish setter. Were the grown-ups with Twila her parents? My grandparents?

The last photo was a large wedding picture. Twila, dressed in white, looked like a princess. A tall, dark-haired, handsome boy looked down at her with so much love I felt a surge of electricity travel through me. It didn't seem possible that people that young could have been my parents.

A knock came on the bedroom door, startling me so much I knocked over the photos. Scrambling to put them back like they were, I stammered, "C-Come in! Sorry!"

The door opened, and Twila stood in the doorway. "You look nice," she said.

"Sorry I took so long," I said.

"Hurry back now, Twila Honey!" called a man's voice from the kitchen. "I miss that pretty face of yours already!"

I grinned at Twila. "How do you do it?" I asked. "I mean, make all those men fall in love with you?"

"All those men, huh?" Twila said. "You've been talking to Colt again, I see."

"I'm sorry," I said quickly. "I didn't mean—"

"It's all right," she said, coming closer to me. She reached up and smoothed back a strand of my hair that had come loose. "I'd say it's a combination of flattery and flirting."

"No wonder I can't get even one boy to like me," I said. "I've never been any good at either of those things."

"It's simple, Sarah," she said. "You just tell a man what he wants to hear, that he's the strongest, smartest, handsomest man you've even seen. And you act like you need him."

"I couldn't!" I said. "I wouldn't know what to say. I get tongue-tied trying to say hello to Colt."

"Actually—and don't tell Colt I told you." She put her arm around my shoulder. "Colt's real name is Calvin Jr. Next time you get tongue-tied around him, remember—he's only *Calvin Junior.*"

I laughed out loud, some of the tension draining out of me.

"Follow my lead." She turned and seemed to float out of the room. I followed.

"Woowee! I am blinded by the light!" exclaimed the man who must have been Calvin Sr. Except for early signs of baldness and what Maggie calls "middle-aged spread," he was a grown-up version of his son. He wore dark brown pants and a dark green, silky shirt.

"Sarah Coop, meet Calvin Cleveland the First," Twila said.

"Two raving beauties!" exclaimed Calvin Sr.

"Did we get lucky, or what, Colt?"

I knew my face must have turned redder than my dress. All I could manage was a nod.

"Not bad at all," Colt said, coming closer and eyeing me as if he'd never met me before. "You clean up mighty fine."

"Calvin," Twila said, "a handsome man like yourself deserves the best a lady can offer." She dished up rice into a fancy silver bowl. "You've been working out, haven't you, Cal."

I caught Calvin sucking it in as he smiled at Twila.

We walked into a huge dining room I hadn't seen before. The long, white linen-covered table was set with real china and glasses cut like diamonds. Maggie's family drank out of glasses like this, crystal. There was more silverware set out for the four of us than Dotty had in her whole kitchen. I wouldn't have any idea which fork to use.

Twila slid by me, and without so much as a glance, whispered the answer to my unspoken question. "Start with the outside fork and work your way in."

Colt pulled back my chair and seated me. He took the seat beside me. He smelled like leather. Every girl in my school would have died for him. *Calvin Jr.*, I thought. *Calvin Jr.*

Calvin Sr. set down two goblets of what looked like white wine. I lifted mine and sniffed.

It smelled like the real thing, but what did I know? Dotty never brought home wine from the Hy-Klas. I'd probably smelled the stuff all of two times at Maggie's.

"There you go, little lady," said Calvin Sr. "Nothing like a fine glass of good wine to take the edge off."

18

Colt took several sips of his wine. "It's good, Dad," he said.

I turned to Colt, amazed. "Are you drinking age?"

Calvin Sr. nearly choked on his wine. "The boy's not even driving age!"

"You're not?" I asked, totally confused. "I thought you were older. You can't drive yet?"

"Not for a year," Colt said, taking another sip of his wine. His dad filled Colt's glass from the green bottle.

"Not that being only 15 has kept Colt from driving, you understand," Calvin Sr. said, punching his son lightly in the shoulder. "This one keeps me on my toes!"

"Dad!" Colt scolded, but he was laughing too. "Some buddies and I got in a little trouble hot-wiring cars and taking them for drives, just for kicks," he explained.

"Without asking?" I knew it was a stupid question as soon as I'd said it.

"That's why we hot-wired," Colt said. "It saves the trouble of asking."

Twila came back in the room. "Calvin, are you giving that boy a hard time about test-driving those cars?"

"Nah," Calvin said. "I was just teasing."

Teasing? I couldn't even imagine what Dotty would do if she caught me hot-wiring somebody's car!

"Well, you better not be hassling him," Twila warned, taking a sip of wine from her goblet. "You don't want to be like *my* father, do you?"

"Why not?" I asked so softly I didn't know if she'd heard me or not. She didn't answer right away. I wondered if it was my grandfather, my real grandfather she was talking about.

Calvin Sr. patted Twila's hand, then answered for her. "Let's just say that Twila's daddy wasn't exactly the forgiving kind."

"You're not trying the wine, Sarah?" Twila sounded disappointed. "It really won't hurt you."

I lifted the glass to my lips. The alcohol smell was stronger than manure. I must have made a face that said what I was thinking because they all laughed.

"How old did you say you were?" Colt asked.

"Fifteen," I said, setting the glass back down without taking a taste.

He leaned over and whispered, "I would have guessed younger."

Twila asked Calvin Sr. to give her a hand with dinner. Colt and I sat in silence as they laughed and cooed from the kitchen. Twila giggled. "Why, Calvin Cleveland! You stop that." But she didn't sound like she meant it. I tried not to imagine what they were doing and not to look at Colt.

"Here we are!" Calvin said when they finally came back to the table. "Let me take that for you, Twila Doll." He set down a huge silver platter covered with a dome lid, the kind I'd seen on TV when butlers served the rich and famous.

"What would I do without such a strong man to help me?" Twila said, handing over the bowl of rice for Calvin to set down.

Dinner smelled faintly barbecued, with a spice I didn't recognize. Twila stood by her chair until Calvin pulled it out and seated her. She touched his arm lightly as a thank-you, and he puffed out his chest again.

When we were all seated, I closed my eyes for the prayer. Nobody said anything, so I opened my eyes. They were all staring at me.

"Are you okay?" asked Calvin Sr.

I felt as if I'd just spilled spaghetti on my lap. I could have said that I was just saying grace. Instead, I said defensively, "I'm okay."

"Do you have a headache?" Twila asked.

"Probably all that wine you've been sniffing," Colt joked. And the awkward moment passed.

As Twila dished up what she called Mongolian barbecue, I shot off a quick prayer. *Thanks for the food, God. Amen.* It wasn't one of my better prayers. But God would understand. I thought about Dotty at home with B.C. What would Twila and Calvin and Colt think if they eavesdropped on one of my aunt's dinner conversations with Jesus?

Twila served us a full six courses, each one better than the last. At the end of the meal, she got Calvin to carry out a mountain of ice cream she called Baked Alaska, and she set it on fire. It was the best dessert I'd ever eaten.

I paid attention to every bit of Twila's flattery and flirting. I would have given anything to have Calvin Jr. look at me the way Calvin Sr. looked at her. The meal was almost over, and I hadn't even tried a single flatter or flirt.

I took a deep breath. *Calvin Jr. He's just Calvin Jr.* "Colt," I began, "what is that handsome actor's name, the one who stars in all those movies? You look just like him, you know. But I suppose you get that all the time."

Twila's nose crinkled, and she nudged me under the table. She approved.

So did Colt. Right away he named some actor I'd only heard of from Maggie. Dotty never let me go to any of the movies the guy starred in. "You really think I look like him, Scoop?" Colt asked.

"Except," I said, drawing it out, feeling his full attention like I'd never felt before, " ... of course ... you're in much better shape—probably because you work with horses and he just memorizes lines."

For the first time, Colt's best smile belonged to me. It was the smile he'd used on the pretty blonde when he'd helped her dismount. Twila was right. This wasn't so hard. I tried to think of something Colt could help me with, the way Twila always asked Calvin for help. "Colt," I said, gazing into his deep, brown eyes, "I wonder if I could get you to help me with something."

"Sure!" he said, his voice eager.

"Well, I'd like to work with Misty tomorrow and get him used to plastic and other things he might shy at. And I need to work on turns and backing. But even a foal can put up a struggle sometimes. It would be great to have strong arms like yours around, just in case."

"No problem!" he said. "I'll come out tomorrow afternoon."

Absolutely amazing. I wouldn't really need his help, of course. But I could always pretend I did.

I asked Colt to help me clear the table (making sure he carried all the heavy trays). When I walked back to the dining room to ask if I could put the china in the dishwasher, Twila and Calvin Sr. were kissing—kissing like I'd never seen two real people kiss. I stood in the doorway, frozen to the carpet, until Colt put his hand on my shoulder.

"This is our cue to go outside," he whispered.

Colt and I walked outside. The night had turned chilly, and stars blinked all across the sky.

"You're all right, Scoop," Colt said, slipping his arm around me and squeezing my shoulder.

I shivered. "Thanks," I said weakly, staring up at the sky, a breeze making the leaves rustle in the darkness.

"You were different tonight—and not just the clothes." Colt leaned into me so close I could smell his Baked Alaska. He closed his eyes, and I saw that I was about to be kissed. All I could think of was what I'd just seen in the dining room.

"See that?" I said, pointing to the sky, where stars grouped themselves in shapes Maggie and Jen and Travis and I had picked out dozens of times. "That one's Orion. Look! You can make out his belt there, and even his shield." I felt Colt's fingers play with my braid. "And that one over there, the one that looks like a squashed M—that's Cassiopeia." I was chattering like

B.C., like Alvin the Chipmunk after 10 cups of coffee.

Colt didn't look up at the squashed M. He kept staring at me. "All I want to see are the stars in your eyes," he said. "You're beautiful in the moonlight."

Me? Beautiful? Did he mean it, or was Colt just flattering me the way Twila had flattered Calvin Sr.—the way I'd flattered Colt? I didn't know what to believe.

The front door slammed, and Calvin Sr. stormed out and stomped off toward his fancy, black car. "Colt!" he shouted. "Get your a— over here right now! We're going home!"

"Uh oh," Colt said, taking his arm from my shoulder. "Looks like it's going to be a rough drive home."

Surprisingly, I felt relief when they'd gone. I wasn't even disappointed when Twila didn't come out to say good night. I used her office in the barn to change back into my jeans. In the bottom of the Hy-Klas bag was an empty pickle jar. I pulled it out. Dotty had thought to stick in an empty jar so I could collect air from Cherokee Bend.

My grandad had started the tradition I was carrying on for him. For over 50 years, he used empty glass jars to capture the air from important days in his life. After he died, I discovered his collection of air from the day he got married, the day his wife died, the day his son, my adopted dad, died, air from wars and days with nice sunsets.

Already I had a good little collection of my own, air from days and moments I didn't want to forget. But this didn't feel like one of those moments, not yet. I put the jar back in the sack.

Twila had set up a cot for me in her office, but I dragged it into the stall where Orphan and Misty were bedded down. The horses nickered to me when I joined them. I fed Misty a bottle and made sure I had enough milk to get us through the night. I set the alarm Twila had given me so I could wake up every hour. The barn sang with horse music—the swishing of tails, an occasional drum of a hoof stamping, horse snores and late night discussions.

Lying on my back, watching Orphan lick Misty's withers, I felt the most at home I'd felt all day. I knew just where I stood with horses.

19

The night went pretty smoothly. Every time I got up, Orphan was there keeping a watchful guard over Misty, who spent most of the night lying in the hay. He drank a little more with every feeding. If I couldn't get Queenie to let Misty nurse by Monday, Twila would probably switch Misty to a store-bought milk-replacer. But I'd still get mother and foal together, no matter what it took.

The last time the alarm woke me, it was just starting to get light outside. Sunlight peeked in through a crack under the barn door. If I'd been at Horsefeathers, light would have criss-crossed through cracks between nearly every board, shooting in long, dusty streaks like laser beams.

I got up, pulled on my sweatshirt, and let Orphan and Misty out into the small pasture. Sam, the morning hired hand I'd met the day before, came and did chores. He fed the horses and opened stall doors. He reminded me of a stick figure, all arms and legs, a man of very few words.

Queenie stayed close to her sorrel gelding buddy, never giving so much as a look to her baby. I watched the sun rise over a hill that grew brighter and greener with the morning light dancing on wet blades of grass. The chill made me shiver. I sneezed three times, so loud several of the horses stopped grazing to look at me.

"Bless you!" Sam called.

Bless me? I'd completely forgotten what day it was! This was Sunday, and I hadn't even said good morning to God.

Sorry, God, I prayed. *I forgot this was Your day.* An emptiness grew inside of me as I pictured Dotty singing her off-key hymns around the house and B.C. griping that he had to slick down his hair.

I raced back to the cot and pulled Dotty's Bible out of the plastic bag. Old church bulletins slid out when I opened the Bible. Every page had Dotty's chicken-scratch handwriting in the margins and between lines. The pages fell open to Romans, probably because Dotty still had last week's church bulletin wedged there.

I read the verse she had circled in red ink: *But we ourselves, who have the firstfruits of the Spirit, groan inwardly as we wait eagerly for our adoption as sons.* —Romans 8:23. I remembered that part of Pastor Dan's sermon because of the word "adoption" and because of what Travis had said about it.

I felt as if I'd been *groaning inwardly*, waiting to find my *real* family. I wasn't sure what it meant about waiting eagerly for adoption. I wished Dotty had been there to ask.

Dotty had a note I could read in the margin: "Get to Ephesians 1:4–5." I turned there and read: *In love He predestined us to be adopted as His sons through Jesus Christ.* There it was again—*adopted*.

I tried to pray about what I'd read. I knew Dotty would have been able to explain it. She never went to college and didn't do that well in high school, to hear her tell it; but she can understand the Bible better than anybody I know.

I tried to sing a hymn in my head, but it just wasn't the same as hearing B.C. fake the words and pretend to follow along, or listening to the Hat Lady hold on to the last note of the song until everybody else is done and sitting down—like she doesn't want the hymn to end, ever, and she's doing her part to make sure it won't.

I'm sorry I didn't make it to Your real house this morning, Lord, I prayed. *Thanks for getting Misty through the night. Take care of B.C. and Dotty. Help me know if Twila's my real mother. And thanks for going to all the trouble of writing about adoption in the Bible.*

The dinner bell clanged from the ranch house, and I ran in for breakfast. As soon as I opened the door, I smelled blueberries.

"In here!" Twila called. She was in the kitchen, wearing a white terry cloth robe. Her hair hung down straight past her waist. "Hope you like pancakes."

"Thanks," I said, taking a seat on the wooden stool she had pulled up to the end of the counter. I knew Dotty and B.C. would eat Korny-flakes or Tastee-O's for breakfast.

She dished me out a thick blueberry pancake that filled my plate. It was the best breakfast I'd ever eaten. I'd almost finished with the first pancake before I realized I hadn't prayed for it. *Thanks for the pancakes*, I prayed hurriedly and silently, my mouth full of blueberries.

While I ate, Twila sipped coffee from a white mug she held in both hands. She seemed to be staring at me. I would never have a better time to talk to her than this. My stomach stopped all business, and the pancakes sat where they were in mid-digestion.

"Thanks for making pancakes just for me," I said.

"I enjoyed it," she said, picking up the newspaper and folding it in half.

It wasn't fair for her not to know about me. Maybe her unforgiving father made her put me up for adoption. Or maybe, said the other side of my brain, I was wrong and she'd never done anything of the kind.

I took a deep breath and squeezed my fork so hard my fingers hurt. "Twila, I'm adopted."

She set her cup down. "Did your aunt adopt you when your parents died?"

"No," I said, not looking at her. "They were my adoptive parents. They adopted me when I was 3 years old." I wanted to look her in the eyes, to see if I could read anything there, but I couldn't.

Finally she asked, "Was it hard ... being an adopted child?"

Was she feeling guilty? "Not so bad," I said. I waited for her to say more. I waited for *me* to say more.

"Are you done eating?" she asked, taking my plate and walking it to the sink. "Misty will probably be waiting for you." She rinsed my dishes, stuck them in the dishwasher, and left. I heard her bedroom door close.

I sat there stunned. Had she rushed off, or was it my imagination? Was talking about adoption too hard for her? Both sides of my brain kicked in with full force: *She knows, but she won't admit it! She has no idea, and you're dreaming again, Indian Princess!*

I dragged back to the barn, feeling a homesickness I don't think I'd ever felt. Misty and Orphan trotted along the paddock fence. I walked to the big pasture, where Queenie and her gelding were grazing. She let me lead her in by the halter all the way up to the paddock. As if Orphan understood what I was doing, she met us at the fence. Misty followed her, prancing all the way up to his mother.

As soon as Queenie caught sight of Misty, the mare put her ears back and showed her teeth. I let her go back to her buddies. Poor little colt. I wondered how he felt being rejected by his mother again and again and again.

On second thought, maybe I knew.

I fed Misty and tried not to think about anything except horses.

"Scoop?" Twila was standing inside the barn. She had her jeans and boots on. "I was wondering. ... Would you like to go for a ride?"

And just like that I believed all over again that I had a real mother. While Twila got her horse ready, a beautiful buckskin quarter horse, I brushed Orphan and bridled her. She didn't want to leave Misty, but I talked her into it.

Twila was waiting for me in front of the barn, but she hadn't saddled her horse yet. "Are you ready?" she asked. With one smooth motion, she swung herself up on her horse bareback. "Hope you don't mind if I ride Rocket bareback."

"Mind?" I couldn't believe it. I *always* ride bareback! It's the only way to ride.

She took off at a dead gallop. I leaped onto Orphan's back and galloped after her. Wind splashed my face like ice water. Cattails and wild-flowers flew by in colorful blurs. Grazing horses lifted their heads as we raced by. It was the ride of my dreams.

She liked to ride bareback. My mother liked to ride bareback. What other proof did I need?

20

At first we rode almost side by side, the wind blowing our braids like horses' tails, straight out behind us. But something happened—or didn't happen. I didn't hear the horse music. That's what Maggie and Jen and Carla and I call the almost musical way the wind works, the heavenly sensation we get when we ride.

When I could, I tried to look into Twila's face. At first her wide eyes said she was loving the ride. But her expression changed to something like boredom.

"Let's go back," she said, pulling her buckskin to a halt and pivoting toward the stable.

We cantered most of the way back, walking the horses through the last pasture, which really wasn't enough to cool them down. Orphan whinnied frantically to Misty back at the ranch, and the colt squealed back to her.

Colt was waiting for us when we got back. "Hey!" he called as we rode up. He took Twila's reins as she slid to the ground. "You guys looked great out there. That's nice riding."

Twila shrugged and glanced back at me, not even seeming to see me. "What time is it, Colt?" she asked.

"Almost noon," he said.

"Put Rocket away for me, will you? I've got a date." She hurried off to the house.

I watched her go, my heart in my throat. If she'd said anything to me, I think I would have broken down and bawled like a baby.

"What's wrong?" Colt asked.

He was staring at my face and I realized my cheeks were wet. I wiped the tears with the back of my hand. "I don't even know if ... if ... if Twila likes me," I said, not willing to tell him what I was actually thinking, that she *had* to like me, that I might be her very own daughter.

"Don't take it personal," he said, his arm sneaking around my shoulder. "Twila just doesn't like kids. That's all. Not that you're a little kid or anything," he added quickly, hugging me to him. "That's why she hires me to teach the lessons. You can see what a great rider she is. She'd be an awesome teacher—but she can't stand to be around the kids."

"She likes you," I said, looking up at him. His face was so close to mine, I smelled his cologne, his soap, his shampoo and hair gel. I let my gaze drop to our feet.

"And she likes you," he said. "I mean, she likes us in a way. She wouldn't like hanging out with us or anything." He chuckled. "I think you know the kind of people she likes to hang out with." He nodded at a green convertible pulling up the drive—Twila's Sunday Man, no doubt.

Twila ran out of the house and jumped into the convertible without opening the door. She had changed into jean shorts and a green shirt, as if she wanted to match the car. She stood up in the convertible and waved to us. "Help yourself to whatever you find in the fridge!" she shouted. The car started up, throwing her back down in the front seat and making her laugh wildly.

I wondered if it was a fake laugh or a real one, if the guy knew, or if Twila even knew. Wriggling out of Colt's hug, I said, "I have to feed Misty." He followed me to the stable, and I gave the foal a big bottle of colostrum.

Colt hung around and watched as I did the next level of imprinting with Misty. I got him used to the crackle and feel of plastic by gently rubbing a little piece of plastic all over him.

"This will help him not be afraid of things that blow in his path," I said, trying to think of something to say whenever I remembered Colt was still there. "He won't shy at everything that moves when he grows up," I explained.

Colt nodded, but he didn't ask questions. Misty let me pick up his hooves with no struggle at all. I pressed lightly on his chest, while pulling gently on his lead rope. In three tries he learned to back up for me.

I'd been so intent on the way Misty was pro-gressing, and so baffled by Twila, I hadn't even noticed that Colt was losing interest. He leaned against the fence, throwing pebbles into the drive. I'd completely forgotten about pretending to need his strong arms.

"Listen," he said, glancing at his watch, "I kind of promised the Lawsons I'd drop by their farm. Their daughter takes lessons here, and one of their mares is about to foal."

I wondered if their daughter was the blonde I'd seen Colt with Saturday. "Will you stop back later?" I asked.

"I don't know. Maybe." Colt walked off. I knew he wouldn't be back later.

Eventually I got hungry enough to go inside and make myself a tuna sandwich. It felt lonely to eat by myself. I wondered what Dotty and B.C. were eating—probably chocolate pudding.

I thought about Lefty. I'd hardly seen the little filly since I'd been at Cherokee Bend. Twila had turned her out with her mom in the back pasture. I headed out on foot. I had to keep reminding myself what day it was. It didn't feel like Sunday. I wondered what B.C. and Dotty were up to, what the sermon had been about, if Carla had gotten Ray to go to Sunday school with her again.

I found Lefty and her mother grazing side-by-side next to a pond. Lefty trotted up to greet me, and so did Dream. You could see how much they loved each other. Why hadn't it worked like that for Misty and Queenie? It didn't seem fair.

~~~~~~~~~~~~~~~~~~~~~~~~~~~~~~~

The green convertible was parked in front of the house when I got back to the stables. I wanted to go inside and call Dotty. And I had to work out with Twila how to get Orphan back to Horsefeathers and who would take over with Misty while I was in school. But I didn't want to go inside while Sunday Man was there.

The sun set, and the air grew colder. Finally, the blond man walked down the front steps of the house with Twila. They were laughing together. I wondered if Twila's laugh was real, or just another case of flirt and flattery. I was so tired, I wondered if anything was real.

Twila spotted me and seemed to just then remember I was there. "Scoop!" she called.

I walked over to meet her in the driveway.

"I talked to your aunt," she said.

"You did?" I couldn't imagine that conversation. "When? What did she say?"

"She agreed that you could spend one more night here if I got you to school on time. Would that be all right with you? I've got Sam coming in to take over with the feedings during the day. If you'd rather, I can take you home now." Twila looked as if it didn't much matter to her one way or the other. She'd asked me if I wanted to go home—*my* home, not *her* home, not *our* home.

"I can sleep in the barn," I said.

"Good. You can wear something of mine to school." She turned to go. "You can shower in the morning, all right?" She didn't wait for an answer.

I passed a long, lonely night in the stable. I loved being with Orphan and Misty, but it felt like I had a hole inside of me. I wasn't sure if the hole was from Twila or from Colt, or from something else. I missed Dotty and B.C. I hoped he'd gotten his math done. On Sunday night, Dotty reads the obituaries to find out who died. She prays for all the families, even though she doesn't know any of them. I never thought I'd miss that, but I did.

~~~~~~~~~~~~~~~~~~~~~~~~~~~~~~

In the morning, breakfast was set out for me in the kitchen, but Twila stayed in the back of the house while I ate. On the drive in to school, she hit me with a new proposal. "Scoop, how would you like to take care of Misty at Horse-feathers for a while? I was thinking, if we moved Queenie there too, you might have a better chance of getting them together. Her buddies won't be around, and maybe she'll accept Misty. You'd have until Saturday, when I need to face the Knowltons. They're going to want to see Queenie as a money-making broodmare."

It was a good idea. It made sense, and I

wanted more than ever to get Misty together with his mother. But it meant I'd be spending less time at Cherokee Bend. "Whatever you think," I muttered, without looking at her.

"Good. If you meet me at Horsefeathers after school, I'll bring Queenie and Misty and Orphan back in the big trailer. Queenie can ride by herself in front." She pulled up at West Salem High School.

A long wolf whistle greeted me as I stepped out of Twila's Jeep. "Great car!" Brian, our star athlete, called. It hadn't even registered that I'd been riding in it. Maybe I was just too confused to care.

"Great dress!" Jessica, Brian's new girl-friend, called.

I waved a thanks and scurried inside. I'd taken one step through the door when I was sur-rounded.

"Tell us everything!" Maggie squealed. "Did you come out and ask her? Did she know? Did you tell her?"

Ray and Carla didn't say anything, but they looked as eager as Maggie. I got out of the door-way, but they followed me, and we ended up in the locker corner of the east hall.

"Look, guys," I said, "I just don't know. Okay?"

Maggie cocked her head to the side, like she didn't believe me.

"Seriously, Maggie," I said. "Sometimes I'm sure she's my mother. We rode bareback. I saw a wedding picture. I know her father didn't forgive her for running away after graduation. But then I think it's just too big a coincidence, like I'm dreaming the connection and she's no more my mother than Dotty is."

Jen had been hanging back from the pressing crowd around me. Maggie turned to her. "Jen," she cried, "tell her! You have to!"

I watched Jen's eyes shrink to dots of blue behind her glasses. She stepped close to me, so only her armload of books separated us. "Scoop," she said slowly, "I've been doing some research on the Internet. Travis says I have been living in cyberspace. At first I wasn't getting anywhere, but when Maggie told me you were in foster homes, well, that narrowed the search."

Jen was a genius on the Internet. She could track anything. I couldn't move. I couldn't speak.

"I did adoption searches statewide, then countywide, cross-checked in hospital records I probably should not have been able to access— but I read how these hackers in New Jersey—"

"Jen!" Maggie shook her arm. "Get to the point!" She turned to me, no longer willing to wait on Jen. "Scoop, Jen found Twila. She's really your birth mother."

21

M aggie!" Jen scolded. "How could you say Twila is her mother? All I said was that I'd narrowed the possibilities!" Jen turned back to me. I still hadn't moved. Jen had been the voice that weighed in with the side of my brain that argued against Twila being my mother.

"Listen to me, Scoop," Jen said earnestly. "Okay. I admit I *did* find Twila, and she did have a baby *about* when you were born. But it proves nothing! I also found about 90 other women who could just as easily be your birth mother.

I was grinding my teeth so hard they hurt.

"Scoop," Carla said, "even if Twila is your mother, she probably has no idea you're her daughter."

"Carla!" Jen cried. "Not you too!"

The bell rang, but none of us moved. I couldn't, and they wouldn't, not until a hall monitor made us. Twila Twopennies had had a baby about the same time I was born. Maggie was convinced that Twila was actually my mother.

I thought about it all day. At lunch Maggie and Jen plopped their trays across from me. "Maggie 37 Brown," Jen said, "I could go home and run another computer search right now, find a different hospital server, and come up with twice as many candidates for Scoop's birth mother—three times as many!"

"I don't care what you find," Maggie insisted. "I know what I know."

I filled them in on the way things were at Cherokee Bend and the way things were with Queenie and Misty. "Sometimes I think," I said, when they'd finished eating and my lunch still sat untouched on the tray, "I think if I could show Twila that Misty and Queenie can bond, even though they didn't at birth, then she and I can do it too. Is that crazy?"

"No! It's beautiful!" Maggie said, wiping away a tear with her napkin. "You can do it, Scoop! And we'll help. We'll get that mare to love her foal, and Twila won't be able to miss the point."

It felt good to be surrounded by my friends. None of them had even mentioned Maggie's Mother's Day parade, and I appreciated it. I knew they were all working overtime to get ready for Saturday.

~~~~~~~~~~~~~~~~~~~~~~~~~~~~~

After school I walked to Horsefeathers wondering if I could look at Twila the same way. But

I didn't get the chance to find out. Orphan and Misty were already in the pasture, nickering to me when I came up the lane.

Travis' pickup was parked out front. Travis strolled out of the barn and waved. "Good thing I stopped by," he said. "I don't think Twila could have gotten that mare unloaded by herself. Cute colt though."

"Twila's gone already?" I asked.

"Yeah. She said she'd call you about Saturday ... and good luck. You'll need it! That mare bares her teeth whenever the foal gets anywhere near her. I put her in the paddock by herself and gave Orphan and Misty the near pasture. Is that okay?"

"Thanks, Travis," I said, trying to figure out if what I felt was relief or disappointment.

Travis and I tried for two hours to get Queenie and Misty together, but the mare reared and tried to bite Travis twice. Finally we gave up. I fed Misty Foal Lac, milk replacement, and turned him out with Orphan in the back pasture. Orphan seemed to love introducing the new guy to Cheyenne and Moby, who acted like jealous aunts. It was fun to watch them gather Misty into an instant herd.

Queenie, on the other hand, showed no interest in anybody except Carla's horse Ham. They grazed peacefully together, with just the rail fence between them.

~~~~~~~~~~~~~~~~~~~~~~~~~~~~

It felt good getting mobbed by B.C. as soon as I walked in the door. Obviously manic, B.C. didn't stop for a breath until he'd told me all about the church's Mother's Day float, his F on a math quiz (which of course was my fault for not being home to help him study), and the latest episode of "B.C. and Grace ... and Tommy."

Dotty came home early and wasn't much different from B.C., acting like I'd been gone two years instead of two nights. She fed us and raced off to church to work on the float. The foal had been drinking so much Foal Lac at a time, even from a bucket, that I only had to set my alarm once during the night to run down and check on him.

At school, Jen, Maggie, Carla, and even Ray all had their own ideas of how to get Queenie and Misty together. During lunch period I ran to the barn to fill Misty's milk bucket, and that got him through the day. Tuesday after school Jen and I tried using the stalls at Horsefeathers to get Queenie used to her colt. First we put Misty in one stall, with Orphan next to him so Orphan didn't have a fit. Next, we brought in Queenie, who did great—until she caught the scent of her foal. Then she kicked her stall and escaped to the paddock.

Maggie walked to Horsefeathers with me on

Wednesday and tried riding Queenie close to her foal. Maggie stuck with it for over an hour, even though I knew she had parade business waiting for her. Queenie didn't appreciate it though. She almost threw Maggie when she got too close to Misty.

Thursday Carla and Ray and I tried brute force, bran mash, oat bribes, and music. Queenie didn't fall for any of it.

On Friday all of my friends showed up at Horsefeathers, and we worked until dark, but it was no use. Queenie didn't like Misty any better than when they were at Cherokee Bend.

"I don't know what else to try," Ray said.

"Thanks, guys," I said, turning loose Queenie's halter. She high-tailed it to Ham, and they whispered together over the fence. "I appreciate all the help. I know you're all busy with the parade tomorrow and everything."

"Are you riding with us, Scoop?" Maggie asked.

Jen elbowed her.

"You don't have to," Carla said. "We understand. I thought Mother was coming in from Kentucky for the weekend, but she phoned last night to say she can't make it."

"I'm sorry, Carla," I said. I knew Carla hadn't seen much of her mother since the divorce. It had never occurred to me that Mother's Day might be hard on her too.

"What are you going to do when Twila comes for the horses tomorrow?" Travis asked.

It was the one question I'd tried not to ask myself. "I don't know. I *have* to get these two together. I figure I'll get one more try tomorrow. Who knows? Maybe Queenie will come through when she really has to. That's all it would take, you know—one time for her to see that having a kid isn't so bad." I quickly added, "For Queenie to see that about Misty, I mean." But they knew I'd been thinking about Twila and me.

~~~~~~~~~~~~~~~~~~~~~~~~~~~~~~~

Saturday morning Dotty and B.C. were already bustling around the house when I came downstairs. "Morning, Scoop!" Dotty called on her way from the kitchen to B.C.'s room. "I can't believe you slept through all them phone calls! You'd think this town ain't never saw a parade."

"Don't come in here!" B.C. shouted from his tiny room. "I'm making a poster for the float. It's a surprise!"

On the kitchen table was a piece of garlic bread from last night's supper. I stuffed it in my mouth, a quick breakfast before my final attempt at making Queenie and Misty a family.

The phone rang. My mouth was full, so I let Dotty get it.

"Hello?" Dotty always sings hellos. "Yes … Well how 'bout you come by the house now?

You can take in the parade. And we can have us a little lunch here first. … Nah! That ain't no trouble! … I reckon … *Brunch* then."

Brunch? Maybe it was the Hat Lady. She probably had fancy meals called "brunch," but she should have known she wouldn't get one at our house.

"That's fine," Dotty said. "See you in an hour then. I'll tell her." She hung up.

"Tell *who,* Dotty?" I asked, swallowing the last cold, greasy bite of garlic bread.

Dotty lumbered to the sink, opening and closing cabinets. "Where did I put them Kleenex? Uh—tell *you,* Scoop. I'd lose my head if the good Lord hadn't saw fit to hook it to my neck."

"Tell me what? Who was on the phone anyway?" I had to get going. I wanted to have Misty and Queenie in the paddock together when Twila arrived.

Dotty found her Kleenex, then turned to answer me. "That was Twila Twopennies. She's coming over for brunch."

22

Dotty!" I screamed. "That was Twila? *My* Twila? Why didn't you get me?"

"She never asked for—"

But I didn't let her try to explain. "You invited her *here*? For lunch? Here?" I couldn't believe this was happening.

"Well," Dotty said seriously, "Twila called it *brunch,* and I kind of went along."

"How could you, Dotty?"

"I thought you'd like having her over, Scoop." Her bushy eyebrows met above her glasses. "I know how much you like them people at that ranch. I just thought—"

But I wasn't listening. My mind was racing in a million directions. "What will we feed her? Did you think of that? We don't have anything to eat!"

"I could cook us up toasted cheese. I got us that sliced orange cheese B.C. likes so much. What do you call it?"

"No!" I shouted. "That's not good enough. We need ... cinnamon rolls ... and fruit ... and juice. What could we make little sandwiches out of? Maybe bacon? No. Not bacon. Ham?"

"I reckon I could make a run to the Hy-Klas," Dotty said.

"Yes! Go, Dotty! Go now. Hurry! And get *real* coffee."

She reached behind her and untied her apron, revealing black slacks too small for her and a plus-sized white T-shirt.

"Are you wearing that?" I asked.

Dotty looked down at herself as if she couldn't remember what she had on. "I reckon I could change if you—"

"Wear the navy dress you wore to Grandad's funeral, okay? But you better hurry. Twila could be here before you get back!"

"That Twila,..." Dotty said, looking away and pushing her bangs out of her eyes, " ... I reckon she's a fine dresser."

I rubbed at something sticky that refused to come off the table. "I don't know. It's not so much the clothes. It's more her style. Everything she wears looks awesome."

"I see," Dotty said softly.

The last thing I wanted to do was hurt Dotty's feelings. "You look great in that navy dress, Dotty!" I said quickly. "It looks good on you."

Dotty was already halfway to her bedroom, so I couldn't be sure she heard me. "I better git," she said, her back to me.

In the living room I raced from chair to couch, picking up newspapers, books, jackets, shoes. Then I tossed them into B.C.'s room.

"Hey!" B.C. protested.

"Twila's coming, B.C.," I explained. "You have to be really, really good. Don't eat with your fingers. And don't ask her dumb questions."

After Dotty left, I dusted with one hand and vacuumed with the other. Since I didn't have time to mop the kitchen floor, I wiped it clean with a dishrag. The counter was cluttered, and I arm-swept everything into a drawer. Next, I set the table, trying to remember how Twila set hers. We didn't have four matching anything, so I gave the best plate, the only non-plastic, un-chipped one, to Twila.

"B.C.!" I yelled. "Do we have any straws?"

Twila and Dotty walked in at the same time. I shoved my rag under the couch cushion and met them in the doorway. "Hi, Twila!" I said, holding the door open.

"I was just telling your aunt she shouldn't go to any trouble." Twila's gaze darted around the room, as if she were on the lookout for creatures lurking in dark corners.

"We can eat fast and get over to Horse-feathers," I said, hurrying her out of the living room.

Dotty followed us and plopped the Hy-Klas bags right onto the table I'd set. "I reckon we *oughta* eat fast. B.C. and I gotta get to our float for the parade. Scoop, why don't you take Miss Twopennies up to see your room?"

"*Twila*, please," Twila corrected.

I could have strangled Dotty! I hadn't had time to clean my room, my tiny attic room, which was about the size of Twila's bed. "I don't think Twila wants to see my room," I said.

"Sure she does!" Dotty insisted. "This girl has more horses in her room than you have at your ranch!" She turned in the general direction of B.C.'s room and yelled, "B.C.! Come help!" To Twila and me she said, "Go on! B.C. and I will get that brunch set out."

Leaving Dotty and B.C. seemed like the lesser of two evils. Twila didn't touch the banister on the way up to my room. I turned on the horse lamp on my dresser. What was there to see? A roof shaped like the letter *A*, horse posters, an unmade bed? I caught Twila frowning at the nearly dozen glass jars that sat on my dresser, jars filled with air of days I wanted to remember as long as I lived. Twila looked right past them and didn't ask.

She pulled my feather out of the plastic vase on my dresser. "What's this?"

"That's a horsefeather," I said. She looked sideways at me, and I went on. "Carla gave it to me before I had the stable. It's really a cuckoo feather."

"Why a cuckoo feather?" she asked, putting it back in the vase and wiping her hands on her jeans.

I could remember the day Carla gave it to me as clearly as if it had been yesterday. I'd been at the lowest point of my life—afraid I'd lost Orphan, the barn, and everything I cared about.

"Carla says cuckoo birds lay eggs but don't want to raise their babies. So the mother cuckoo carries the egg all over until she finds the perfect nest. She sets it carefully in the nest and then flies away. When the chick hatches, it's raised by whatever bird is on the nest."

"I never heard that," Twila said. "But why did Carla give it to you?"

"Carla knew I was adopted," I said, not looking at her. "She gave it to me so I wouldn't feel so bad about ending up in another nest, I guess. It was like a symbol that Horsefeathers was where I belonged." I hadn't thought about that story in a long time.

"Scoop! Lunch!" B.C. yelled up. "I mean *brunch!* Hurry! We'll miss the parade!"

Twila looked as relieved for the excuse to leave my room as I was.

Dotty and B.C. were arguing at the table when we came down. "I wanted you to wear a hat in the parade!" B.C. whined. They'd left the best seat for Twila and the next best for me. Dotty had set out a plate of ham, a loaf of bread, jars of mayonnaise and mustard, oranges and apples, cinnamon rolls, and a carton of grapefruit juice.

B.C. took Dotty's hand and reached for Twila, then pulled back. He and Dotty closed their eyes, and Dotty prayed: "Jesus, we thank You for brunching with us and bringing Miss Two—, that is, Twila, here to share our food, even though they was out of them chocolate donuts B.C. likes, but we're mighty grateful for all You give us."

I peeked at Twila. Her head was bowed, but her eyes were wide open, still scanning the room for monsters.

"Help that there mama horse to make nice with her baby," Dotty continued. "And thank You, Lord, for Orphan, who's acting like just about the best mama there ever was, if You ask me, although I know You don't need to ask nobody. Help yourself!"

"She means *you*," I whispered to Twila. Dotty passed her ham, and B.C. shoved a package of rolls that claimed on the plastic wrap to be cinnamon, even though they looked like a big rectangle with thin white glue poured over the top.

"You know," Twila said, glancing around the table, "I'm really not very hungry."

"Me either," I said.

"Look at them two, will ya, B.C.?" Dotty

said, slapping two pieces of ham on her plate. "No wonder they's so skinny. See if you can't pass them some rolls there."

B.C. picked up the rectangle of rolls again and started to pass it, when all of a sudden he dropped it on his plate and yelled, "Yuck! Oooo! Ants! Ants!"

I saw them the same instant my brother screamed. Tiny, black ants crawled up one side of the rolls and marched in formation down the other side. Other ants looked stuck in the gooey frosting.

B.C. hadn't stopped screaming, "Ants!" Twila looked scared to death of him.

I jumped to my feet and pulled back Twila's chair. "We have to go now," I said. "B.C. is just talking about his *Aunt* Dotty ... and ... and his other aunt. He gets really excited about them. So I think we should leave."

I didn't need to convince Twila. We were out of the house in two seconds flat, and halfway to Horsefeathers in her trailer before either of us spoke. I didn't know if she'd seen the ants or not. Either way, it was a brunch she'd never forget.

Twila's long fingers drummed the steering wheel. "Scoop, it must be hard for you, living there."

"It's not so hard," I said, wondering what she meant by it. "Dotty and B.C. are okay. You just caught them on a bad day."

She parked, and we got out next to Horse-feathers paddock, where Queenie was grazing alone. "Where's the colt?" Twila asked.

"He and Orphan are over there," I said, pointing to the pasture where Misty lay in the grass, with Orphan standing close by.

"You mean Queenie still isn't accepting her foal?" Twila sounded disappointed, and kind of angry. "The Knowltons are meeting me at the ranch this afternoon, Scoop."

"It's okay!" I said, praying it would be okay. "I think Queenie will make up to Misty this morning. I really do. Just wait a minute, and I'll try them again."

She peeked at her watch and sighed. "I guess you can try again if you hurry."

I hurried. With a whistle, I got Orphan and Misty to meet me at the gate. But I needed Twila's help. I wanted her to be in on this. "Twila, will you lead Queenie toward me when I say so?"

While she snapped the lead rope on the mare and waited, I slipped Misty's halter on and snapped his lead. He pranced behind me, and Orphan followed. "Stay, Orphan!" I commanded. "This is between Queenie and her mother."

Orphan pawed the dirt and nickered to Misty, but she obeyed.

"Now!" I told Twila.

We led our horses toward each other, mother and foal. My heart was beating so fast I hoped I didn't upset Misty. "She's your mother, Misty," I said. "It's going to be okay."

Far away I heard band music start up. A loud speaker blared garbled words. The Mother's Day Parade was in full swing.

We were 10 feet apart now. Nine. Eight. Seven. Six. It was working. Four. Closer than Queenie had ever come to her foal since birth. Three more feet and they were there. Misty wanted it. I could feel his excitement.

Suddenly Queenie jerked. Twila didn't expect it. The rope slid through her fingers. Twila stumbled. The rope smacked in the dirt. Fast as a bullet, Queenie wheeled around and kicked. I screamed as I saw hind legs and two hooves headed straight for Misty.

23

Before I knew what was happening, a blur of black sailed by me. Orphan threw herself in front of the foal. Queenie landed both back hooves square into Orphan's side. My stomach ached at the sickening thud as horseshoe connected with flesh and Orphan moaned.

"Orphan!" I cried.

"Scoop!" Twila yelled. "Stay back!"

Orphan stood her ground, protecting Misty as Queenie wheeled around, teeth bared and bit into Orphan's neck. Orphan squealed, but she didn't move.

"Get away!" I screamed, shaking and crying. I hugged Misty. He was trembling as we watched helplessly.

Over the paddock fence, Ham whinnied. Queenie turned and looked, whinnied back, and just like that trotted over to him.

I couldn't stop crying. Rushing to Orphan, I threw my arms around her neck. Teeth marks showed in a circle under her mane. I checked her stomach, feeling along her belly where she'd been kicked. Hair was scraped off in a half-moon, but she wasn't bleeding.

"Everything all right?" Twila asked, standing back from us. "It's not too bad, is it?"

"Not too bad?" I said, trying to stop sobbing. Orphan had already moved around to lick Misty. The foal huddled close to Orphan, his tail between his legs.

"Listen," Twila said, "this was a bad idea. I'm sorry things didn't work out."

I'd stopped crying. Fascinated, I watched Orphan nuzzle the foal from head to hoof. She had to be hurting, but all she could think about was the foal.

Twila was saying, "I've got to get the mare back to Cherokee Bend. You did what you could here. It's not your fault, Scoop. Don't feel so bad." She pulled a check out of her pocket. "Here. This is yours. You've earned it." She handed it to me. "The truth is, Queenie just isn't cut out to be a mother."

I studied Orphan with Misty. Twila was absolutely right. Queenie wasn't cut out to be a mother. But Orphan, my Orphan? She and Misty may not have shared a drop of blood or a single gene, but they were family.

Twila was already walking toward Queenie. "So I can come back for the colt tomorrow, if that's all right." She led the mare toward the barn. "Scoop," she said, stopping and looking over at me. "Colt and Calvin are back at Chero-kee Bend. Do you want to come along home with me?"

I studied Twila Twopennies, the way the sunlight made her black hair sparkle. I shook my head. "I *am* home," I said softly.

"What?"

"Nothing," I said. "Thanks, Twila, but I think I'll just stay here where I belong."

Her eyes narrowed and I thought she was about to say something. Instead, she just nodded. "All right then."

I wasn't angry or disappointed. I didn't know if Twila was my birth mother, or if one of a thousand other women was. I'd always be grateful that someone had gone through with her pregnancy and let me be born. And maybe now I understood a little better that whoever she was, she was no more cut out to be a mother, a real mother, than Queenie was. Someday it might be important for me to search on my own and find out who my biological mother really was.

But not today. Today belonged to someone else.

I said good-bye to Twila and told her Orphan and I would take care of Misty for as long as she'd allow us to. I helped her load Queenie and prayed for Twila as she drove off. Then I got the colt settled down, scratching him on his back until his heart stopped pounding.

"I know you don't want to leave, Orphan," I said, as I led her out of the paddock and gently swung up on her back. "But you and I have a parade to catch."

Orphan cantered down Horsefeathers Lane, picking up speed as we headed for town. I thanked God for protecting my horse. She didn't seem to be in pain from Queenie's blows. In the distance I could hear the faint blare of trumpets and the echoes of drums. When we turned onto Main Street, my heart sank. The crowds along the street had drifted away. The parade had already passed.

"Hey there, Scoop!" Mr. Richmond waved to me. He was standing in front of his store, the only department store in town. They sold everything from socks to screwdrivers. "You missed a mighty fine parade. You should have seen Mrs. Powers and Joan and the others on your church float. Their hats were something to see! Your aunt was on there too, in the back, working on something, I suppose. You know your aunt."

I *did* know my aunt. And I knew Dotty would be just fine working instead of enjoying the float she'd worked so hard on. But I wanted more for her today.

"Mr. Richmond," I said, jumping off of Orphan, "I need to buy something fast."

It took the whole check Twila had given me, but I came out with the prettiest orange-flowered hat in Richmond's Department Store. "Thanks, Mr. Richmond," I called, the hat tucked under my arm. There was still a chance I could catch the parade before they got back to the fairgrounds.

Orphan's hooves clopped down Main Street as we galloped after the Mother's Day Parade. It was easy to find them. We followed the drums as the music grew louder and louder.

Finally I saw the fire truck bringing up the rear of the parade. A big sign hung on the back end of the truck: MOTHERS PUT OUT FIRES ALL DAY LONG!

Orphan galloped past the firefighters, through the straggling Shriners with their red hats, past kids dressed like clowns, past the football float, and float after float.

At last I spotted a pink float ahead of us. They were the first float in the parade, with only horses ahead of them. A big sign dangled above the wagon: HATS OFF TO MOTHERS! And on the back, the name of our church.

I urged Orphan up beside the float. "Dotty!" I cried.

Mrs. Powers and the other ladies sat on chairs decorated to look like thrones. They were dressed in formals like prom queens. In the middle chair sat Grace, waving to the few spectators left.

"Hello, Scoop!" called the Hat Lady.

"Have you seen Dotty?" I asked.

Mrs. Powers pointed to the other side of the float. Orphan and I galloped around the front of the tractor that was pulling the float.

"Scoop! You made it!" Maggie cried as I passed her. Carla and Jen and Travis and everybody greeted me.

I waved to them and raced to find Dotty. She was lying on her stomach, flat down on the fake float floor, reaching over the side of the wagon to hold up one end of a banner that had come unhooked. Pink Kleenex lay scattered around her, and B.C. was holding onto her ankles so she wouldn't bounce off.

It was so ... so totally *Dotty*, I felt a lump in my throat.

"Scoop!" B.C. yelled. "You came! Did you see Grace? Dotty invited her and she came! We passed Tommy Zucker and you should have seen his face!" He let go of Dotty's ankles to make a funny face.

"Help!" Dotty cried, as she started sliding head-first over the edge of the float.

I reached down from Orphan and pushed Dotty's shoulder back up onto the float. B.C. ran back and pulled her legs. Dotty rolled over, then got herself to a sitting position. She was laughing so hard, she couldn't get words out. Her glasses hung crooked from one ear.

Orphan and I kept up with the float, right next to it, as it rolled slowly up the street toward the fairgrounds. "Are you okay, Dotty?" I asked. But I could see she was. She just couldn't stop laughing.

"My sign!" B.C. yelled.

I looked down and saw the banner Dotty had been holding up. It dragged in the street. I reached down and with Dotty's help stuffed it back in place. Sitting back on Orphan, I read the sign: "AS FOR ME AND MY HORSE, WE WILL SERVE THE LORD!"

"I spelled *house* wrong," B.C. said sheepishly.

"You did just fine, B.C.," I told him. The verse said it all. I was home. This was home. And Dotty and B.C., and I, we *would* serve the Lord.

"Is that cute little colt all right?" Dotty asked, almost toppling over when the float wagon hit a bump.

"Did his bad mommy take him home?" B.C. asked.

I shook my head. "Nope. Turns out his mommy wasn't cut out to be a mommy, B.C. Orphan and I will take care of him though. Don't you worry."

"I been wondering, Scoop," Dotty said. "How much you figure a little bitty colt like that would cost?"

"Dotty?" I said, hope springing up inside me. "Do you mean—?"

"I reckon B.C. here could use a colt of his

own. There's a lot he could learn from taking care of it." Dotty smiled so big at B.C., you could see where she'd lost a tooth.

"For me, Dotty?" B.C. cried. "My very own horse! Wait until Grace hears this!" He ran over to tell her.

"You reckon we could pay a little bit out of each paycheck?" Dotty asked.

"I reckon," I said. "Dotty, I'm sorry about everything, about brunch, and being at Cherokee Bend so much, and missing church last Sunday." There was a lot more I wanted to tell her, but I couldn't get the words to line up right.

"You're thinking Twila might be your mama, ain't ya, Scoop?" she asked softly.

I jerked back as if Dotty had thrown something at me. I hadn't said anything like that to her. Not even once did I think she was on to my suspicions about Twila. But I should have known. Dotty is so close to God that sometimes I think God lets her peek into my mind.

Finally, I nodded. "I was thinking that, Dotty. But I don't think so anymore. I don't know who gave me birth, but I do know she wasn't cut out to be a mother. And I'm okay with that. What I do know is that my home is here with you and B.C. You're all the mother I need."

"Thank You, Jesus," she said, without taking her gaze off me.

Suddenly I remembered the hat still tucked under my arm. I handed it to Dotty. "Happy Mother's Day," I said.

"Scoop! For me? Why, it's the most beautiful hat I ever seen!"

"Put it on!" B.C. shouted. "Put it on!"

Dotty put the orange-flowered hat on her head slowly, as if it were a crown. It was bigger than her face. The brim covered her forehead. The flowers on it clashed with her dress and the float. But she looked beautiful to me.

"Dotty!" the Hat Lady shouted. "We made a seat for you over here! Hurry up now! The parade's almost over. And you need to show off that fine, fine hat."

Dotty looked up at me. "Lord, thank You for this here family You give me! Thanks for this here hat."

I wasn't sure if she was thanking God or me for the hat, but it didn't matter. I was thankful for all of it, grateful to be where I really belonged, strangely more sure than I'd ever been that this was my home.

Dotty waved to the crowd as we pulled into the fairgrounds. She tipped her brand new hat. I rode up and joined my friends, pulling Orphan to the front, between Maggie's and Travis' horses.

"Everything turn out okay?" Maggie asked, her forehead wrinkled in concern.

I nodded. There would be plenty of time to tell her more.

"I'm glad you made it," Travis said, sounding like he really meant it.

"Me too!" said Maggie 37. "Especially since I know how much you hate Mother's Day."

I glanced back at B.C., who was sharing a chair with Grace, and Dotty, who was waving with one hand and holding onto her hat with the other. Tomorrow, on the *real* Mother's Day, B.C., Dotty, and I could walk by Horsefeathers on our way to church so I could capture the air of home and family. What the three of us had was something deep, deeper than bone and thicker than blood.

"Mother's Day isn't so bad," I said, "Not when you're home."

Saddles

Western (Stock Saddle)

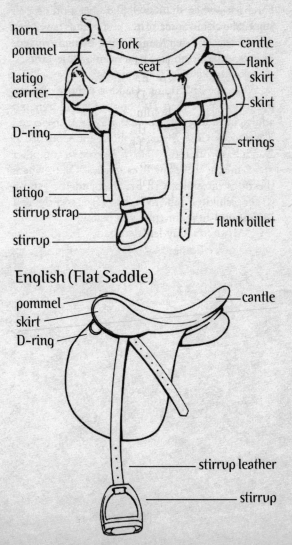

horn

pommel

fork

latigo carrier

latigo

stirrup strap

stirrup

D-ring

seat

cantle

flank skirt

skirt

strings

flank billet

English (Flat Saddle)

pommel

skirt

D-ring

cantle

stirrup leather

stirrup

About the Author

Dandi Daley Mackall rode her first horse—bareback—when she was 3. She's been riding ever since. She claims some of her best friends have been horses she and her family have owned: mixed-breeds, quarter horses, American Saddle Horses, Appaloosas, Pintos, and Paints.

When she isn't riding, Dandi is writing. She has published more than 200 books for children and adults, including *The Cinnamon Lake Mysteries* and *The Puzzle Club Mysteries*, both for Concordia. Dandi has written for *Western Horseman* and other magazines as well. She lives in rural Ohio, where she rides the trails with her husband Joe (also a writer), children Jen, Katy, and Dan, and the real Moby and Cheyenne (pictured below).